RiPPLE 2020

A Kingston University
Student Anthology

RiPPLE 2020

A Kingston University
Student Anthology

First published in 2020 by Kingston University Press

© Copyright lies with the individual authors.

The moral rights of the authors have been asserted.

All rights reserved.

No part of this publication may be reproduced or transmitted,

in any form or by any means electronic or mechanical,

including photocopy, recording, or any information storage

and retrieval system, without prior permission of the publisher.

Every effort has been made to fulfil requirements

with regard to reproducing copyright material.

The publisher will be glad to rectify

any omissions at the earliest opportunity.

These stories are works of fiction.

Any resemblance to real persons living or dead is purely coincidental.

A catalogue of this book is available from the British Library

ISBN 978-1-909362-50-5

Typeset in Bell MT, Corbel, Elephant

Cover photograph © Robin Hutchinson

KINGSTON UNIVERSITY PRESS

Kingston University

Penrhyn Road

Kingston-upon-Thames

KT1 2EE

Twitter @kingstonripple

Instagram @ripple_kingston

The Team

Managing Editor
Paige Mader
Head Of Communications
Ed Rowbottom
Editorial
Aifric Kyne
Alexane Rondolat
Amanda Zazueta
Jocelyn Pontes
Manasvi Pawaria
Maria Omena
Noemi Vallone
Rachel Sexton
Raluca Lupei
Santhini Koshy
Marketing
Alexane Rondolat
Amanda Zazueta
Destynee U Oakley
Gabriella Buckner
Melissa Malec
Tiffany Cook
Production and Design
Amanda Zazueta
Casey Gibson
Kaniz Sukaina Husain
Lisanne Hopkin
KUP Supremo
Emma Tait
Special Thanks
Robin Hutchinson & The Community Brain

Contents

A Note From The Editors
Foreword

Part I : Changing Rooms

Part II : General Submissions

A Note From The Editors

We the editors are proud to present to you the 16th annual edition of the RiPPLE Anthology. For us, the greatest pleasure is in being able to showcase Kingston University's wide and diverse range of talent.

This year, the anthology contains selections from two parallel competitions. The first asked writers to submit works on the theme 'Changing Rooms,' inspired by RiPPLE's partnership with The Community Brain. We feel so deeply honoured to have had their support this year and, in turn, to be able to do our small part in raising awareness of their mission to bring life and pride back to Tolworth, in part through their initiative to restore the King George's Pavilion changing rooms.

The second was an open call for general submissions. For this competition, writers were invited to submit pieces on any theme or topic of their choosing. As a result, we received such an exciting variety of works, which we hope is reflected in this anthology.

Although we wish we could have published everything we received, we are very excited about the selections made here, and strove to publish the very best Kingston University's creatives have to offer. And with that in mind, we hope you enjoy what we have made.

With many thanks,
The RiPPLE Team

Foreword

Settled in an area of playing fields in Tolworth lies The King George's Pavilion changing rooms. Proudly opened in 1962, the pavilion has since fallen on hard times and its once modern design now lies neglected and vandalised. It appears as a ghost of what was; a memory of a different time when the playing fields buzzed with the sound of sport and civic pride was to be applauded. And it asks a question: what role and what purpose will 'changing rooms' play in the future?

The Community Brain, a local organisation founded on the belief that everyone is brilliant if they are given the help and support to be brilliant, has developed a fascination with the potential of this building. How can it regenerate itself to provide a new community asset; a new place of change? Yes, of course that can mean physical change for sport, but can it also be used to change attitudes? To change awareness? To change lives? Can it positively affect people's relationships to where they live? The Community Brain's SHEDx - Growing Ideas in Tolworth, wants the local communities to help answer some of these questions.

It was with these thoughts that our conversations with Kingston University and the RiPPLE team started. What does 'changing rooms' or a changing room mean to people? We are delighted to have been part of the RiPPLE process and we hope that some of the pieces in this publication might just help to effect change for some.

Robin Hutchinson &
The Community Brain

Part I

Changing Rooms

Changing Rooms

Dannielle Sadiq

As a child, you did not connect the events that took place in these rooms with the unravelling of your life. But when the pieces of your mind were restored, you understood that these rooms (seen and unseen) were the root of the pain that once left you broken. You call them "the changing rooms." You once sat in each of them, waiting for instructions on how to live.

You are ready to revisit the rooms. The rooms that brought shelter to your body and mind, and the ones that witnessed the bruises that painted your skin like a patchwork.

The Kitchen

Four walls; seeping with patches of mint and cream colours. One section of this room was decorated with a wallpaper that had small images on, yellow ducklings, yellow flowers, perhaps, but you have blocked that out. You think about the time you and your sister watched the dry wall create air pockets, making the wallpaper peel, pop and bubble. The two of you scratched away at it. Off-white tiles plaster the floor and the browning skirting boards cover the corners of the kitchen. They held the russet cupboards filled with mismatched plates and cooking utensils. You remember how the tiles felt on your sensitive soles when winter came, the chill that shot up your spine, forcing you to bend your feet to their sides. The countertops were glossed with a rich black cut marble. When they were first plastered in the kitchen, you smelt the clean-cut freshness of the minerals that split the kitchen in two as it sparkled whenever the sun greeted it.

Then, your mother cooked most of her husband's meals here, Jamaican cuisine to accommodate their married life. Smells of fried fish, plantain, rice and peas, curry goat and ox tail filled the house. You said you detested your mother's newfound cooking, rich with foreign oils, spicy sauces and tender meats. You said this, forgetting that you are also half Jamaican. Back then most of your meals came from the side cupboard; inside there were the cheapo 55p pastas, tinned foods, crisps, biscuits, breads and your favourite value branded cereals. You lived on these cereals for years, along with British foods seasoned with pellets of black culture. Fried chicken with homemade wedges, 'just like the fish and chip shop' you said, spicy spaghetti Bolognese and macaroni and cheese made with a spoon full of ketchup.

In the kitchen, you ate alone, mostly staring into the garden in awe of the tree that stood there. You laughed at the thought of a Chinese cherry blossom resting in such common grounds, the pink petals fell in autumn creating a sea of magenta. Back inside the kitchen was a long oak table that had four chairs, here you sat with your older sister, your mother and your sweet father. You watched your mother re-marry in the garden as you stood beside the marble in the kitchen.

You remember things changing, all at once and quickly. At first you adapted well to this change; you even rubbed the hairy man's chest as he replaced your father. But as you grew, you and your sister began to fear this man. From the kitchen, you watched as his tools broke branches off the cherry blossom tree; his hands dampening the magenta petals, turning them into ash. Soon, you and your sister were the only ones who dined at the oak table. Even though she suffered at the man's hands too, she kept you safe, wrapping you tight with her softness. Over time the kitchen became broken, tired and dirty and the man began to beat you both. The cupboards became unhinged as they witnessed this and the skirting boards fell at the sounds of your screams. One day they refused to stand and hold the broken kitchen up any longer.

This kitchen became the first changing room: it moulded you. So, you took all of the stored goods and began to feast on them, day and night. And as you blocked out the world, you felt the abundance of rolls that stuck to your back, a sagging of your arms and a newfound roundness to your face. You dwelled in this place until you were full and moved onto the next room.

The Body

The walls of the next changing room are made by those layers of fat that overlapped one another. This room was a gift, something that developed from small cells inside your mother's womb. *Ibukun*, yes, your body is a blessing.

This room was your body, the one that you built for yourself. Here, you spent your days, months and years in shame. You hid from the world and covered yourself in layers of clothing until you began to blend in with the rest of the world. You grew scared of your body, looked at how your stomach stuck out, the way your black skin was now painted with stretch marks in odd places and how your knees buckled under the pressure you had burdened them with. You obsessed over your body and took to the scales often. Undressed, you waited to see the number of pounds you had accumulated. 23 stone was your heaviest. The sight of your body began to make you feel sick. You had strange visions of taking scissors and cutting away the pieces of fat that served you no purpose. You wanted to do this but failed many times, only letting the scissors scratch the surface of your skin.

As you began to cocoon yourself, you tiptoed to the kitchen where the man continued to break you. He beat you, took away the foods that you lived off and allowed words of disgust to roll off his tongue.

After a while, you realised that the man's words had no power over you. But as you reached adulthood, you still heard the words the man spoke of as you walked past shop floor mirrors. You used social media to compare the thickness of your thighs with others and punished yourself by withholding food for days. Your body grew tired of the punishments you put it through. You were known to occasionally binge, pinch and scratch your skin until it became numb. You lost weight, lots of it but still, you weren't happy. You gained some of it back, and still you weren't happy. Soon, you realised that your happiness was not attached to your weight and you began to stop punishing your body. You relaxed in it, you liberated it, you even took care of it.

Now, you smile at the sight of your body; embracing the blessing that it is.

Darkness and Light

The walls in this room are fluid; they are not seen but can be felt. In this room, you have been known to open the doors that lead to darkness. You have spent many years, perhaps your whole life, wandering in-between the doors of life and death.

But the thoughts that filled your consciousness as a child were different; these thoughts were of how your teddy bears would grow old with you, how your primary school hamster would not die and how you would stay six forever. You could taste its innocence; sweet like rhubarb.

But as you grew, you spent too much time in the room of darkness, you heard the tricksters and the thoughts that chuckled while you sat in your sadness. These were the thoughts that fed you lies of how man-made pain could heal the brokenness that spread throughout the soul. They told you that pain was the only feeling that you could experience in this lifetime, and at times, you believed them.

The mind was infested with depression and anxiety, something that lingers like a shadow. It told you not to eat, sleep, pray or seek help, so you did nothing. But its effects on the body couldn't go by unnoticed. You began to cry more, but in public and this was something you tried hard to fight. You cried on trains, trams, buses and planes as you suffered.

You remember the month of April 2017 as it was the month where you thought of every possible way of how to kill yourself. You thought about the pain you had endured in your short lifetime; how impossible it was to silence your mind and how unfair life had been. You wrestled with these thoughts for 28 days and on the 29th you began to walk beside the canal river. As the sun shone on your back, perhaps a simple offering of warmth, you shrugged it off and began looking into the river. Still heavy, you began to think of your sister, and the pain she had also endured. You thought about how your death would be the undoing of her life, you thought about your father and how he would become a broken man and you thought about how helpless your friends would feel if you passed on.

And because the pain of the people you loved broke you even more, you spoke against the noise in your mind. You screamed, you swore and spat at the thoughts that consumed you. You sought out help and sat in a velvet covered chair and spoke your truths out loud. The darkness tried to take control, but things became brighter. As the darkness left, you changed. You began to venture out in your mind, expand in your thinking, and as a result, you saw life in colour.

There are no bolts or locks in this changing room anymore, in fact you have access to every room now. The one where you think of the future is your favourite one by far. But most days, you dwell in the rooms that flicker creativity; they thread like unbreakable gold in your mind. On the days when you think back to the first room you still cry, in fact, you howl. But you choose not to stay there. On the days where your mind tells you that your body is too much for this world, you poke and prod at your skin and say, 'I am alive'. And on the days where your mind tells you that you are not enough, you silence it with your own voice.

The kitchen, your body and your mind have all evolved. You see this most in your smile, the days when you sing in the shower and when you look into the mirror and speak softly. And so, you continue to grow with a collection of keys, holding access to the changing rooms that no longer have power over you.

Out on Parole

Gabbi Buckner

The mattress sprawls naked in the corner of the room
like a body stripped down to the skin
and scoured into something clean and cold
under the lamp of a mortuary table.
Plaster flakes like a scab around the
holes from posters and paintings
where I tapped nails into the wall
with the cautious edge of a book
so the Queen of the Duplex down the hall
didn't dole out commentary
like a bowl of hot soup for the homeless
about my decorations ever-changing.
A week in the local Stanford Prison Experiment
and I was playing the favorite to get a few hours
of yard time in peace
from a warden I knew was my equal but
who pet my head and cooed of my delinquency,
her project to rehabilitate
into the Greek life through frat parties and blind dates,

and I slit my wallet open
and let her bandage me up in the latest fashion,
and drowsy with the drug of a sorority girl's approval,
I floated into my nine by ten cell and smiled
as the lock clicked.
Larger and larger doses each week and I shoved my
furniture from wall to wall
to dress the cell anew and stop the growing tolerance—

until after seven months there is nothing left to change
and I speed away with my cardboard boxes and mattress
to a room with no holes, where I can hammer in
my own again.

But when I close the door at night,
I wait for someone to turn the key
and each moment unlocked I feel an itch on my chest
like an old scab
and I pick at the brown crust
and it opens.

keep your coat on.

Chrissie Joslin

sour milk drips
through   cracks   in lips
a pageant slip
a kiss-me-quick
turned

                  s   l   o   w.

tidal   w   v   s
        a   e   flow
 like
fingers d
     o
     w
     n my throat
keep your coat
on.

last night's attempt still lingers
on your cuffs

pockets stuffed
with lungs
silent   hums
are easier to swallow.

rotate your head 360°
you were always
handsome   from behind
eyes
like tiny shrines
pierced to make the **b**
                    l
                            u
                        e run dry
till all you see
is
me.

I use my hair as a weapon
threaten
you
with
femininity
my dignity
tied in a knot
around your tongue
each strand
a **comic sans** plan

and just like that
i've won.

Next.

Changing Room

Imogen Loth

The relentless burning below suddenly subsides. Oxygen slaps my flushed face and rushes up through my nostrils. Finally I can breathe, finally it's over. My eyelids flutter closed, then open sharply as a high-pitched squawk sears through my skull. Terrified, I drag my eyes away from the stained ceiling and stare down between my legs.

Its blue face contorts into a menacing scowl while its pink limbs jerk and stretch. A tacky yellow wax sits in the folds of the arms and gathers under the armpits making me gag but I can't look away now. It's like when you drive past an accident on the road; you can't help but drive slowly, hoping to catch a glimpse of a mangled body in amongst the wreckage.

Now awake and cold it opens its mouth wider, revealing gums and a bright red tongue. Its lip and chin quiver making as much room as possible to let out a piercing yell. The vibrations of the cry hypnotise me and I just stare.

I don't feel anything. I don't feel sympathy, let alone love. I have no desire to reach down and pick it up, nor do I care to wrap it up and make it warm, but just in case God is watching me,

I unbutton my cardigan and slowly tug it off my body. I pick up the screaming thing and drape the cardigan over its body, but it doesn't stop crying. Its skinny legs punch the cotton creating momentary mounds while its face grows redder and more distressed, but I don't care. I just simply feel empty, alone. My heart is devoid of love; you know, that love that mothers are meant to feel all consumed by after the birth of their precious babe. I don't feel anything though, and instead cut the cord, place it on the top step of kind Mrs Wilson's house and shuffle away.

It'll never remember that first half hour spent with its mother, nor will it remember the sweat and blood engrained into the changing room walls. It will never remember what I looked like, the emptiness clouding my eyes. I will remember though, remember it all.

As I limp along the path up to my house, I look up at the sky; it is nearly dawn. The clouds are tinted orange and drift slowly across the moon, creating thick shadows to my left. I walk with my shadow until I reach the front door and we depart, thankful for the company. I haul my shaking body up the stairs and into bed, yet, just as I'm about to drift into unconsciousness, I stop myself.

I didn't even check if it was a boy or a girl. I wait for the sadness, regret even, to filter through but nothing comes. Instead, I turn my head to face the rising sun.

When It Rains, It Pours

Klara Armstrong

It was expected
Much like dominoes
When one falls
The whole thing collapses
And much like myself
The mind plays tricks
I notice the swift change in my mood
My inability to sleep or get dressed
or leave the warmth of my bed
The lack of energy to even watch Netflix
You see when it rains, it pours
Depression swallows me whole
and oxygen escapes me
I have to remind myself how to breathe
Even putting one foot in front of the other
Seems an impossible feat
It's always a full-strength attack
Without warning my mind decides
you're going to suffer tonight,

tomorrow and the day after that
with no end date in sight
It could be weeks or it might be months
You might lose the will to live
But it gets better
That's what everyone will say
But when it rains, it pours
and I feel like I'm drowning
Well intentioned words of comfort wash right over me
When it rains, it pours
But when the sun shines
I know I'll find myself walking from the waiting room
to a doctor's office
then head straight to the chemist
Prescription in my pocket
Opening another door
Changing rooms
S u r v i v i n g

Shock

Clara Tamez

It would be a shock to discover I'm perfect.
I'm sweating in front of a silent fridge
denying the need.
For someone to go find me another subject.

The back of the fridge used to go unchecked.
I ate a moldy cookie that flaked off
in my dripping mouth.
It would be a shock to discover I'm perfect.

Even your husband says he loves your intellect.
All fucking is fighting with no
lights so he can fantasize
about someone else. Go find me another subject.

I have pink streaks of pressed in fingerprints on my neck
from sharp smelling lotions trying to suck
it back in and compromise
on it being a shock to discover I'm perfect.

The mirror is a liar and that makes me one too, I suspect.
My squatting legs ache but the dimples
still smile on my thighs.
Someone go find me another subject.

I'm old. My feet crack and leave drops
of blood so what should I expect,
to still look like my young self and satisfy?
It would be a shock to discover I'm perfect.
Someone go find me another subject.

But now I know

Rachel Essex

I stumble into the toilet, catching my breath from the overwhelming heat of the crowded dance floor. Vomit fills the air, heightening as I tumble inside the empty toilet. I run my hand along each crimson wall to steady myself, thinking about how much they must have seen. My eyes are only half open and what I can see is slightly blurry. The end of the wall comes far too quickly and I sharply turn a corner, placing my hands on the dripping counter in front of me for balance. There's a small hope that it's just water, though I've been here enough times to know otherwise. There's a mirror directly in front of me, I can barely make out my own face through the blur. The incessant amount of sweat dripping down my face causes my false lashes to begin peeling from my eyelids. I move my hands to stick the left lash back on, causing me to lose my balance and forcing me to the alcohol-soaked floor, tearing off the one eyelash in the process. Well, I think it's alcohol. I'm too intoxicated to move, so I lay still with my face inches away from other people's vomit and drenched in the booze that they've spilled.

A soft hand gently clasps my own as someone attempts to lift me from the floor. They struggle for a while but after several moments, they succeed. She tells me that I should be more careful, maybe not get so drunk. I comprehend none of that so I grin at her; she knows I'm not listening. My lack of response prompts her to continue talking; it's clear that she doesn't like silence. She tells me her name is Lucy; I'm fairly certain I won't remember by the morning. She probably knows that too. I keep flashing a wide smile at her and grab her face with both my hands, pulling it close to mine whilst telling her how pretty she is and how I think we'll become great friends. A thought passes through my mind; I'm wondering if she knows that the vomit she can smell isn't mine. Thinking out loud is one of my worst drunken habits that I only realise when she laughs immediately in response. I also realise that I've been lingering for a little too long before I drop my hands and pull away. Though, she didn't seem to mind. Before leaving, she asks for my number, she wants to message me tomorrow to make sure I'm still alive. After exchanging numbers, she leaves and I know I'll never see her again.

I have no recollection of getting home or to bed, actually most of last night has disappeared from my memories. All I can remember is a mop of curly brunette hair but I have no idea why. Too much thought causes a pounding headache so I pull the flower covered duvet above my head to block out any light and groan loudly reminding myself never to drink so much again. I repeat that thought moments later when my stomach begins to churn and bile burns my throat. I race to be sick, pulling the bathroom door almost completely from its hinges by slamming into it on my way. I'm desperately hoping but not entirely sure if I'll make it. I do. I walk back to my bedroom, it's chic but small. There's only enough room for a wardrobe, a single bed and a TV but there's a sense of cosiness in its diminutive size. Fairy lights hang at the top of the pale blue walls, photos of me and my friends are scattered among posters of my favourite childhood bands. I smile lightly, thinking of the simpler times.

A loud ping pulls me from the nostalgia and brings my attention to my phone. There are 12 notifications, 11 from various guys from my secondary school who've seen that I don't look like a troll anymore and want to "meet up". We all know what that means. I roll my eyes and keep scrolling through them all without a response until the name Lucy with a heart emoji appears. I click on the notification and open the message, reading a text that says, "Good afternoon, thought you might only just be getting up and didn't want to disturb you. Had to make sure you're still alive". The previous night begins coming back in pieces. As she said she would, she texted me to see if I was still alive. I don't show my surprise, instead I choose to reply with: "barely, my head's so sore, I should not be allowed to drink." Lucy responds: "it's your own fault, you drank too much lmao". The texts flood in one after the other, the exchange continues day and night for over a week, never missing a beat. It feels as though we've known each other forever. Something just feels right.

I'm nervous. I don't know why; I find myself screaming into my empty wardrobe whilst its contents are strewn along the carpet. There's not much time to think about it as she says she'll be here to pick me up in 15. After weeks of texting, we've managed to arrange a date to meet in person. I shove some floaty summer dress on and brush my dark hair, looking down at my outfit before grabbing my bag and heading out to stop myself from changing my mind for the thirteenth time. A small, red Fiesta pulls up outside my house; she waves from her rolled down window and I walk towards the car. She greets me as I sit down and I gaze at her for a moment. I'd seen her photos hundreds of times yet I never noticed how her nose perfectly fits her face or how her cheeks have a tint of pink beneath her bronzer. Her eyes are a light shade of green but they have flecks of gold too. Her lips are slightly cracked but it doesn't stop her from having the most beautiful smile. She asks if it's okay if we go shopping; she needs to buy new clothes and she says she'd love my opinion. I nod lightly, still feeling nervous. A comfortable silence fills the air until she turns the volume up on the radio and we sing along terribly. I instantly recognise that it's Fall Out Boy; their poster hangs on the wall of my room. My nerves begin to ease knowing we have at least one thing in common.

From the moment we step out of the car at the shopping centre, we don't stop moving. She drags me around to every shop we pass. Every. Single. One. It amazes me how she manages to go through at least 15 shops and not buy or try on a single item. Shop number 18 is the lucky winner where Lucy finally finds something she likes. I've never met anyone so picky; I like it though; it shows that she cares and that's something I'm not used to. Once she's chosen all the items she wants to try on, she grabs my hand, intertwining our fingers, and drags me to the changing rooms. My feet are incredibly grateful for the small seat in the corner of the room. I slump into the seat and inaudibly sigh in relief but it's loud enough for Lucy to hear as she laughs. It takes a minute but it suddenly dawns on me that there's only me, Lucy and four white walls pushing us together.

I refuse to look directly at her as she begins to try on the different items, even though she asks for my opinion on each one. Opting to look at the plain door beside me, I give a review of 'Yeah, looks nice' to every outfit she tries on. I watch from the corner of my eye at her pulling up a pair of tight jeans, jumping and wiggling into them to make them fit properly. She wasn't particularly thin but she was nowhere near fat, she had the kind of curves that were hard to get but you'd be lucky to have. She thinks I'm not paying attention to her. There's a light grip on my face, Lucy pulls me to her direction, forcing me to look at what she's chosen. It didn't matter what she wore, although it would not have been my top choice for an outfit, she is easily one of the most beautiful people I've ever seen. She moves her hand from my face, I seize it and pull myself up. A centimetre, that's all there is between us yet she feels so far away. We stare intently at each other for a brief second before my hands grab her face and pull her close, the way I did the night we met. This time, I kiss her.

I'd always had a feeling that I liked girls but I was never sure. People said it was a phase and I didn't really mean it; everyone experiments when they're young and at university. I questioned myself for a long time. But now I know. I found the answer in the changing room of my local shopping centre. All of a sudden changing room had a brand-new meaning.

Changing Rooms

Isabella Ruffatti

I've changed rooms quite a lot. All nothing special. They were rooms I slept in, not lived in.

There's 10-year-old me in my horse-back-riding gear in one of three rooms I had while my family lived in Costa Rica. I can't remember which. It is raining. It rains in every one and they blur into each other. There's only one thing I remember distinctly.

I could not wait to change rooms.

There's 12-year-old me in my new school uniform, a white shirt with a tie, plus the skirt. I'm back in the country I was born in, in a large, old wooden house my mom never liked with its beautiful staircase, rats in the roof and a large library which reminds me of the one in *Beauty and the Beast*.

Friends from before don't know me anymore and a girl I have never met before claims me as her best friend and that is that.

As it turns out, we have plenty of friends in common: books.

I could not wait to change rooms.

There's 15-year-old me in a school uniform I had grown to loathe and an ugly fringe I knew was ugly. My family lives in the shiniest and newest 15-storey building that only lacks a 13th floor. Yet I never felt lower and unluckier. Head against the wall. Head removed from the wall. Head hitting the wall. And repeat. 'You will learn these jokes. Make your friends happy. Make them like you. Or else.'

Later, my cheeks hurt from the effort, the willing them to like me, to see me, to remember me. Cast away like a used water bottle, the school's group of castaways takes me in.

I could not wait to change rooms.

There's 18-year-old me in my green-white graduation dress. The bed is made, as it is every morning at exactly 5:30 on weekdays. I may have hated school, but I hated being late more.

But school is done now. And from behind the closed door of the bathroom, the trashcan full of aborted friendships had started to stink.

I could not wait to change rooms.

There's 20-year-old me in my new summer room, which doubles as the maid's room for the rest of the year, in a new place, Mexico City. It's 7:00 am and I can hear my mom in the kitchen. A door screeches and there's some scuffling, panting. That'd be my dog, Nala, back from her early morning run with my dad. Still too early for a sighting of my sisters. After graduation, this could be my life. Now, I do not quite fit, they'd have to change house.

And I would change rooms.

There's 22-year-old me in my room in Seething Wells, opposite from the room I stayed in during my first year. I fail to recognise the Isabella from three years ago, let alone twelve. I am working towards a degree here, a direction in life. I have met many people I am happy to call my friends.

I will change rooms again. But this time, I'll be leaving a room I won't be shutting the door to.

The Quiet

Zoë Marriott

She pauses in the dark corridor.
The bathroom door is ajar,
And light makes a harsh, blue-ish bar where it seeps around
the edge.
She hears a creak, a clank.
Feeling foolish, calls: 'Hello?'
There is no one inside when she pushes open the door.
The room is quiet now, and dark.
The glow was the streetlight,
And the sounds were only the radiator cooling, the house
settling,
The way that a woman will toe off her shoes,
And slip out of her bra when she knows
That she is alone.

Pirouette

Caitlin Murphy

This room is brighter and airier than the last. It's a welcome change. Sunlight spills in through the windows and for the first time in nearly two weeks, I feel like I can relax. Walking in the never-ending suburbs in summer heat brings bug bites and contentment. The main streets of all small towns feel largely the same; general stores, pharmacies, and artisanal goods. Yet I don't tire of them. People are pleasant and interested, especially if I tell them about the places I have still to see. It's easy to feel settled here. I almost forget the date that I have to move on to the next room.

I find myself treading carefully in the silent hallways. Behind each closed door, people are living and breathing. They are close to each other physically, but the thinly plastered walls may as well be miles thick. Nobody comes here to meet others. It's easy to feel like a ghost in these endless stretches of nowhere. All of the halls sport the same antiquated look — garish carpets and mahogany beams. After nearly an hour of wandering, I drift downstairs to play pinball.

The drive to the next place to sleep is long and isolated. This paved track turns upwards into the mountains, and the woods thicken around me as I go. It occurs to me here that I don't actually know where I'm trying to get to. The next room is a few hours away, the room after that is another long drive away. But once the short stays in different places end, I don't know where I'm hoping to end up. My tickets for the flight home sit printed in my backpack, folded neatly inside my passport. They have been purposefully ignored for days.

When I get to the hotel, nestled just outside of a cosy hilltop town, I can see why this one was more expensive than the last few. Each set of four rooms sits in a separate log building, dotted around the rising landscape. There is a small fire pit in the middle of the yard. The key that I took from the hospitable woman at the reception opens the second door of the cabin at the top of the hill. She told me that she had owned the site for twelve years now, and is just pleased to be able to help people. Everyone passing through has a story.

At the fire pit on the second night, reclining in a deck chair, I speak with a rugged man from Indiana. Like me, he's unused to driving in such thick, forested places. He talks about the close encounter that he had with a moose that jumped out at him. Apparently, they're huge. I've only seen the taxidermized head that lay on the wall of a bar I visited, and he finds that funny. He's up here for business, meeting a potential timber trade partner. The drive so far has taken six days of near-constant travel, but he doesn't like flying. I feel foolish for thinking that I've gone a long way; in comparison, it's like I've been going in circles. We say our goodbyes, and I will never see him again. I spot a small black bear on the edge of the woods when I head back to my room, and I wonder where its mother is.

The car that I've been getting used to calling mine is due back in four days. I've only just got the hang of driving an automatic. It's filled with my coat, my bags, the intricate woven blanket that I picked up from a small-town shop. I'm tempted to stay for a while longer. I could drive across the country, sleeping in the back seat of my car until my Visa expires, and I have to leave. Life on the road. It sounds romantic and refreshing, like a character from an old novel. A part of me dreams of disappearing past the treeline and never returning.

The constant change of room feels like being trapped inside a revolving door. I'm trying to get inside, but I don't know what's waiting for me when I do. I just keep turning and turning, pushing ahead in circles. I hope I'll find what I'm looking for; but perhaps I won't. Wide open spaces lie ahead of me. Hopefully, somewhere in the wilderness of ever-changing rooms, fulfilment will follow.

Between Bodies

Jamie Dawson

I'm somebody between bodies — the shade of sunsets and
peaches between fire and sunflowers, the pause before a leap
into oblivion with uncertainty to cushion my fall, the phase
between phases, one foot in the house where innocence died,
in the room I locked myself inside like a self-contained
prisoner, marking my skin like the flagellants of old, another
in flats, houses, rooms which feel nothing like home, in cities
densely populated, where few know my name and even less
know my story, the **'PLEASE STAND BY'** as viewers wait
for regular transmission with frustration and annoyance; I'm
indecisiveness incarnate — unsure of myself yet pushing
the problem onto the laps of professionals with (hopefully)
more insight than I, my feet guiding me down roads most
frequently travelled, while my mind runs with wolves and
through densely-packed trees; I'm godly and godless — less
than perfect yet created in the image of power and strength,
lacking belief yet wishing to be believed in, abandoned in an
ocean of cryptids and leviathans of monstrous proportions,
desperate for salvation but fearful all the same, what will

happen to me if I die? what will happen to me if I live? does God believe in me? Tell me these things and tell them sweetly, tell them truthful and tell them hurtful; I'm between me and myself — me: the person confused yet knowledgeable, fearful of this information and the power words contain, like Liesel Meminger as she hides a burning book beneath a uniform of conformity and hate, bound by shackles of a society heading for self-destruction, with those in my image as the poster children, myself: a future I fear I won't be around to witness, filtered by a vague sense of hope, a strange nostalgia and sadness unlike any I have ever known, like Susie Salmon (like the fish) as she observes the passing lives of those she loved and loves, clinging to her humanity in every intake of breath, every tangible second, moving from the underground shelter to a hidden crevice in her killer's home, to the blissful paradise of her Heaven, greeted by faces so like her own, with pain to overcome, achievable when I see those whose image I wish to replicate, to imitate, to believe in, I: someone known and unknowable, a byproduct of the in-between, the creator of the in-between, he who inhabit the in-between the way people inhabit any space which has become theirs and only theirs.

I am between bodies, yet I am whole. I am whole, yet I am a million selves thrown to the wind with liberty and excitement. I am here, there, everywhere, yet I am me. I am the in-between, the covert and the overt, the magician of concealment and revelation, the Everyman and the Onlyman. I am real.

The Things in the Attic

Gabbi Buckner

All my friends were jealous of your sloping ceiling like a tent
we would crouch inside on sleeping bags
to hide from hungry bears.
Plywood Cinderella-attic walls,
our witch's cave, our fairy hollow, our tree house
too high for the beasts circling on the ground below.
You were the best thing I owned

but the tree house had a ladder and when my friends were gone
Mommy climbed it
and tore in like a hurricane tidying up a small village
everything in us thrown onto the front lawn to teach a lesson
but all I learned was that I owned nothing
you were the only thing she couldn't break

so you were mine to destroy
with paint black as my new eyeliner
and pushpins stabbed through posters
of bands whose music shredded my eardrums so I floated

deafly away from those lives at the bottom of the ladder
and every year of footfall, every boy I loved and let inside
us, sinking you inch by inch, cracks spreading like tense veins
across the downstairs ceiling that Mom glared up at
like those animals that wait on the forest floor
for you to come down
or fall.

When I visit home, she offers the extra bedroom
which she has made up just for my return,
so much prettier
than your black scarred walls and creaking floors
and the storms she has raged within you.
But she can't clear the wreckage, it is piled
high in the corners of my own mind
and I climb my ladder to sit amongst
the storage boxes and dusty lamps
those unwanted things she's not quite ready to throw away.

The Remedial Room

Morgan Bratli

I must say, I do not remember putting my sock there. I have only the one pair, so why would I not be fully aware of where they are? Dear me, and now its bright red as well! Never in my entire goddamn life have I purchased a bright red sock. They are profoundly ugly, at that. One of those would never be found stuck on my foot! But, then again, it does feel so obvious — and so... naked — when you're wearing just the one. So, I put on the colour of the devil on my right foot, while the left one is the deepest, murkiest black; excellently reflecting how I feel being in this place.

I arrived a few days ago, and already the place makes my eyes want to pop from my skull. How had I arrived here, again? Did I drive, or take the bus maybe? All I remember is going to sleep in a queen-size bed and waking up in a king. A number of oddities have taken place ever since I came here, this I do know. My slip-on shoes have mysteriously evaporated. My nightgown has shrunk two or three sizes, and my toothpaste has become way tangier in taste. The office chair at the desk in my room keeps changing heights of its own accord, requiring me to readjust it whenever I sit down in it, even if I only took a short trip to the kitchen.

Must be my rampant imagination playing tricks on me. No matter — London sure does look beautiful from here, especially considering I can't see it! The fat oak right outside my window is making quite sure of it. I don't even see the faces of her inhabitants, which is no complaint.

When I headed off for bed last night, were not the walls painted grey? Why, pray tell, are they now the most disgusting light beige I've ever had the misfortune of laying my eyes upon! My eyes are burning for heaven's sake!

I walk through the tight hall — hours ago it was even tighter — into the sitting room, passing the blinding white dining table and chairs and continue on to the sombre, all-black kitchen. When I see the fridge, I can't help but let out the laugh that tickled my stomach. The fridge certainly had no padlock and chains draping it as I recall. Now it's all rusted and gross as well. Whatever food has the misfortune of living in there could stay, I have quite lost my appetite.

Kneading my fists over my eyes, I find myself in the sitting room again. And to my profound horror, I find a man sitting on the sofa, with a stupid smile on his rather stupid face.

'Who are you? How did you get in?' I ask.

'Ha! Ha!' he spits, turning his overlarge head to me. 'Why I live here now, of course! Won't you bring me a coffee, please, Mary.' His voice is distorted and static, like he is speaking through a telephone.

'How do you know my — no, you dim twit! This is my apartment, and I will have you get out of it.'

His smile evaporated, and the fat between his eyebrows wrinkled into a bridge. 'I will never leave, and neither will you,' he says in a monotone, robotic voice. 'Ha! Ha! Only joking. Coffee, please!'

I say nothing, wishing the man was locked away inside my fridge.

'Mary. I have an itch deep inside my belly. A coffee itch. Make sure to put more cream and sugar than actual coffee,' he says, with his eyes shot wide. 'In fact! Now I've given it more thought, I'll have just the cream and sugar.'

I can't look at the man with my brow straightened. No ordinary man drinks his coffee without coffee! I want to choke him and toss him out the window and toss the dining table after him. However, I do not think the fall would kill him seeing as we're on the ground floor. He would just plop onto the ground, wouldn't he? At best he will break his little finger. But perhaps the table would kill him? Or should I throw the massive brick of a television chasing after him instead?

I turn away, I can't stand to look at his cream and sugar loving face any longer. 'Please leave. However it is you got in, I do not care, but please, leave the same way.'

'Huh. Now that I hear you mention it, I'm not quite sure how I did get in,' he says with the same jolly undertone in his voice that made my belly churn with nausea.

Out of nowhere, I hear a tiny static voice coming from the man, yet his lips do not move at all. His head begins shaking and he breathes like a galloping horse. 'No-no-no,' he blurts out. 'Let me try again, let me try something else. I'm sure I can come up with —'

He disappears. He does not evaporate or melt, he just disappears, faster than a housefly taking to the air. I'm trying to make sense of what happened, but by God would I be lying if I said I was not profoundly happy by his swift exit.

From the ceiling comes a hellish swathe of metallic noises. The sound materialises into a murmuring chant. A sugary voice with a perfect enunciation of each word it speaks.

'Good morning, Mrs Aurantiaco. How are we feeling thus far?'

'What, who — what do you mean, "thus far"?'

'Mrs Aurantiaco, I am delighted to welcome you to the Remedial Hotel. I am also delighted to introduce you to your very own Remedial Room! I'm sure this may all seem peculiar, but this room and the changes it presents will help us understand the current status of your mental welfare, and furthermore be able to make countermeasures to stabilize it. You see, you are not currently in this room in the physical world. In fact, you are currently under heavy sedation and in a deep slumber. I am speaking to you from the real world, and so was the man you met earlier. What you saw was simply a visual projection that looks nothing like him at all. We apologize for his odd behaviour; his insertion was a bit premature. After all, the analytic review of your mind is still ongoing.'

My stomach is empty, but still I feel like vomiting. My heart begins to pound against my ribs, and under the voice of the sugary man, comes a faint beeping growing faster.

'Now, now,' he continues. 'There is no reason to be alarmed. Your children are very concerned on your behalf, and wouldn't want you to do anything rash. I can assure you; you will leave this place fully healed of your maladies. Now return to your day as you would in the real world, and we will do our work from here. But be warned; you must not, under any circumstances, leave the room. It can be extremely detrimental on your health. Tally-ho!'

I stand still, not even moving my eyes. I don't know for how long. Minutes, perhaps an hour, until a cold draft tickles my cheek. The window has disappeared entirely, and I see only a blue sky with lonely clouds outside of its naked veil. My belly congeals as I peek over the empty sill. There is nothing, there is no ground, no end in sight. The building stretches into terrible infinity. If I jump will I ever meet the ground? I certainly hope so. I don't want to be in this ghastly experiment of a place any longer!

The metallic screech rattles my brain again. This time the voice is low, whispering carefully.

'Apple juice has far more pleasing a texture than orange,' the same man I heard before says before it cuts out for a few moments. '... when she wakes,' he goes on, 'she immediately proceeds to the refrigerator, suggesting her hunger, but then —'

'The padlock and chains. Eating disorder?'

'Could very well be so. And then there's the conundrum of

the different colored socks, which could mean...' he drags the words like he wants for the other man to finish his sentence.

'Disorientation! No, drawing a parallel to imperfection! Yes, poor self-image!'

'Calm yourself, Mr Malum!' he shouts and then immediately lowers it as if a teacher gave him a sour look. 'But I do believe you are correct.'

'Thank you, sir. I mean ... the walls turning beige over grey, could be — no, that's silly.'

'Tell me your thoughts, by all means.'

'It could symbolize a fluctuation in temper. A brighter colour for a brighter mood.' Everything he says sounds like a question.

'That is silly, yes. Grasping.'

'Apologies, sir ... the microphone light is on by the way.'

There's a clatter like a thousand falling spoons which is fast followed by a frail yell.

'Malum, you dunce!' I hear the rolling wheels of an office chair. 'Ha! Ha! Mary! Hello Mary. My assistant Mr Malum here has run into a bit of a technical issue.'

'Wake me up! I don't want to be here anymore!' I yell.

'Mary, please. We have not yet finalized our prognosis. We need only a fraction more time and then we will be able to decide on a course of action.'

'Wake me up, you twit, or I'll leave the room!'

'Now, Mary. That would be very unhealthy!'

The walls begin to foam like the lip of an ocean. The black dining table and its chairs shrink and crumple as balls of paper. Under my feet the floor flakes and the whole room trembles. I see the window, and dart its way. In my ears I discern frantic voices. I hear nothing of what they scream.

With my one red and one black sock, I leap into the wind.

Changing Rooms

Anna Svensson-Stoltz

Concrete walls.
Concrete talks, missing the thoughts.
Mirrors painted a bodily sin.
Shame on me for my body not being thin.
I was young and it was cold up north.
My breasts were bare, not meant for pillow talk.
Grey pants and spots on my face,
a stench of us common people.
No fancy perfume covered us,
No rouge on my face, just magic dust.
I wanted to be just like you,
A thickened skin and lips so lush.
I span by the mirrors, pretending to be free
Before I knew it, adolescence had a hold on me.
The changing rooms changed perception,
Should not have looked for validation.
If I leave you with one thing then remember this;
It is not about what you are,
it is about what you miss.

Ode to the Wedding Apparel

Syeda Taslima Hussain

Blossomed amongst greens, crimsons, and golden filigree
You glorify the feminine purpose of simply being
Intricate florals and paisleys render the bitter-sweet story,
Melodies fill the air as the shehnai is playing
Silken threads from the mill create an opaqueness
You hide your true feelings and colour therein
Dainty folds of scarlet and rose madder reveal
The duties that have to be upheld with every kin!
Your beauty shall be heightened with shyness
You shall have to be obedient despite unfairness
Unfailing smiles will paint the rosiness to keep it real.

Sanguine shades and golden brocades are of a bygone age
Welcome are now tones of mauve, turquoise, and jade
Blushing females, spoilt for choices, trying to gauge
Whether the saree or the lehenga will get them laid!
After all, 'tis the modern epoch of equal opportunity!
Sleeveless blouse revealing a stretch-mark free midriff
Whether the ethnic sarees drape or the exotic lehengas adorn

Changing rooms offer to see if you find it a bit too stiff;
Tassels, preceded by sequenced borders for sitting pretty,
You are the showstopper for ongoing hospitality —
The Dupatta signifies the perfect look — happy yet forlorn!

Fresh, delicate roses and white, fragrant lilies engulf the nuptial air
While it lasts, my dear! Enjoy eating pilau rice and succulent curries,
Bangled hands caress curls and twirls of delicately coiffed hair
Mirthful girls rushing out to grab some MacD's and MacFlurries
Who knows what lies ahead after the perfect wedding outfit?
Meticulous silver lacework incarcerates the guileless bride,
You capture her with your expensive, sartorial array
But she's happy to oblige as you are her ultimate joy and pride
'Can't wait to to have the permissible tete-a tete!'
Wholeheartedly, the Possessor of the Wedding Apparel will submit.
 Alas! Can life ever untether from your omnipotent play?

The Ground Change

Sanket Alurkar

The door opened into a room; employees worked at their desks. The girl walked in with a sense of purpose and urgency amidst the rapid-fire clicks of keyboard keys. "It starts here!" a board read in the hallway as the girl took a right towards her workplace at WeShare co-working space. Sophie sat at her desk placed in a semi-cylindrical hollow. Sophie Rehbein, sports journalist with *The Sportz! Magzine*, had won the Journalism Diversity Fund in 2015 and had received the Sports Journalist of the Year award from The Sporting Foundation. She had dark eyes, blond hair, was beautiful and had a way with words.

She got ready for the day; she fired up her laptop. Just then she received a call.

'Yeah... sure. I will be there in a minute.' She closed the laptop and went quickly to the editor's office; Mr John Morgan.

'May I come in sir?' Sophie asked with a voice that meant business.

'Yes, Sophie, I have a new assignment for you! You have to write a story about a historical ground in and around London that has been left neglected over the years. It should talk about the history of the ground, why it was constructed? And one standout feature of the ground,' Mr Morgan said, being right on the money.

'Okay, how should I select the ground?' Sophie asked.

'You can choose a ground that had a rich heritage, but now due to ravages of time is near shut down. The Ground People, an NGO that revives the old grounds, approached us and have asked us to cover the story of one such ground that requires urgent revival or else it would be lost in the sands of time,' Mr Morgan said.

'Okay, I will start the work right after completing my previous article,' Sophie said as she went out of Mr Morgan's office.

'Cool! And keep me updated!' Mr Morgan said.

Images of a charity match between Kingston Renegades and Surbiton Knights were clicked in bursts at the local sports ground in Kingston. The cameramen sat in a row just beside the boundary of the square. The football crashed into the goalpost; that's when Theo clicked an image of the goal.

I have to cover a story about an old and historical ground around London. Call me back when free.

- Sophie.

The match ended in a draw as both teams played their best game. Theo Newman, the man behind the lens, a freelance photographer, had worked with numerous magazines and newspapers. He had a varied portfolio.

'Hi, Sophie! I am at the university ground at Kingston. I saw your text. I wondered which ground you have selected for the cover story. How may I help you?' Theo had called Sophie to understand the assignment. Theo believed in sublimating personal ego for cumulative success.

'Theo, I thought about that and I was confused about how to select from the buffet of grounds. I figured you might help me with the selection,' Sophie said expectantly.

'Hold on for a second,' Theo opened his schedule from the daily planner. 'I have a match scheduled at the Metrodome stadium in Surbiton tomorrow, one of the oldest in the area.

It was founded in 1972. It was designed by Mr Edward Wintringham who has built a string of stadiums in and around London. You can join me tomorrow at 9'o clock in the morning.'

'Okay cool! I will be there.' Sophie said and thanked Theo over the phone.

Amidst the clouds, the sun shone. Mist laden on the field scattered the sunlight. The field sparkled, the birds chirped and a football zipped past the field. The ball shattered the blades of grass that danced to the tunes of wispy winds. Shaun Abbott, university football sensation, winger of the Jaguars, ran with the ball. He tackled the fielder on the turf and broke through the defence. He stood a few yards away from the goalpost. He could sense the defenders coming from behind to take the ball away. He extended his right leg, swung it in an arc and kicked the ball in the goal post that left the goalkeeper stunned and the crowd in raptures.

Theo clicked photos as Sophie sat in the stand that was open in the stadium. The rest of the stadium, along with the pavilion, was closed down long ago. The final of the Unifield cup between the Jaguars and Asteroids had been a roller coaster ride. Both teams played with the motto of "attack is the best defense", and produced a gem of a match. The Jaguars took the game away by Shaun's last-minute primal screamer. The Jaguars huddled up together while the Asteroids were handed a defeat.

Shaun with a big smile said, 'Good game team.'

Amidst shake of hands and back slaps, Shaun went up to his counterpart Russell Harmon and said, 'Well played. You almost had us.'

'You won't get past us next time!' Russell said as he walked away.

'We will see about that,' Shaun said with a wink.

The players dispersed out of the university grounds and walked into the clubhouse. Theo and Sophie sat in the reception of the Clubhouse. They both got up as the players made their way.

'Can I have two minutes of your time?' Sophie asked as Shaun walked past the reception. 'Yes, sure!' Shaun said as he stopped.

'You had a good game,' Sophie applauded Shaun.

'Thanks! It was a collective effort.' Shaun waved to his teammates to go ahead.

'That's fantastic! I am Sophie Rehbein and he is Theo Newman. We want to cover a story about the Metrodome stadium. Would you mind answering a few questions?'

'Yeah, I am cool with it.'

'Can you introduce yourself and tell us what's the one thing that makes you come around to the stadium and play?' Sophie asked as Theo recorded.

'I am Shaun Abbott, skipper of the Jaguars. I play as a winger. I feel the ground here is open and the breeze that flows across makes you want to play for hours.' Shaun looked back at the ground, which was some distance away from the clubhouse.

'That's wonderful! And can you tell us something about the pavilion?'

'It's nowhere near a colosseum but when the crowd gets cheering, it leaves your heart pumped up and adrenaline-infused, in your veins you are ready to go.'

'Now tell us something about the changing room,' Sophie said.

'It has been closed long ago. The players generally use the locker rooms in the clubhouse. But honestly, I would want the changing rooms back at the stadium. Can you write a story that stirs the authority to revive the stadium from its current situation?' Shaun asked Sophie.

'Yes, that's the reason we are here! This story would be published in *The Sportz! Magazine*. Once we convince the authority, the NGO The Ground People would work on the stadium and revive it just as it was in its heydays,' Sophie said enthusiastically.

'I hope you bring back the stadium to its old glory days,' Shaun said.

'Thanks, Shaun, for your kind words. Once again congratulations, you got your team home,' Sophie shook Shaun's hand.

'Thank you so much!' Shaun said with a smile, and went away.

'What next?' Theo asked, as he switched off his camera.

'Mr Morgan told me to talk with Mr George Elliot, Chairman of the clubhouse and sports facilities at the university. He should help us,' Sophie said.

Sophie and Theo went to Mr Elliot's office. It was a spacious office; the walls adorned the trophies in the trophy cabinet, varsity shields hung over the walls like visages of wild animals, a desk covered with important-looking papers, documents, and a laptop. Mr Elliot sent an email. He was in his mid-forties, an alumnus of the university and a former football player. He had a gentle demeanour and was a man of few words.

'Good morning, Mr Elliot! It's a pleasure to meet you,' Theo said warmly.

'Good morning, it's great to have you over. I read your pitch and was intrigued by your idea,' Mr Elliot said.

'Thanks, Mr Elliot, for your compliments. We wanted to interview a coach and understand what he feels about the stadium because we believe that a coach is someone who would be closely attached to the stadium. Someone who would have been an integral part of the team when the stadium was active,' Sophie said crisply.

'Okay, Sophie, I suggest you connect with Mr Robert Schultz coach of the Jaguars team. He has trained the team successfully to five title wins in his career of over twenty years as a soccer coach. You can set up an interview with him. You can meet the man himself who designed the stadium, Mr Edward Wintringham. I will give you both of their email addresses,' Mr Elliot said.

'Mr Elliot, we at *The Sportz! Magazine* are collaborating with The Ground People in a bid to revive the old and historical grounds. The cover story aims to make the authorities aware of the urgent need to revive these grounds,' Sophie said.

'Sophie, that's a big ask, and I understand the nobility of action and purpose, but it would be difficult to promise anything now.

I would suggest you start with the interview and meanwhile I will talk with the higher authorities,' Mr Elliot said, contemplating.

'Thank you so much that would be a great help. One more thing, Mr Elliot; we would like to have the interviews within the changing room,' Sophie said.

'Why?' Mr Elliot asked with surprise.

'We want to capture the spirit of the game and we believe that it all starts in the changing room,' Sophie said emphatically.

'Fair enough! I will make the arrangements,' Mr Elliot said.

Sophie went back to her office and Theo went to cover another match. She wrote emails to both Mr Schultz and Mr Wintringham. Mr Elliot sat in his office as he called the Chancellor of the university.

'Hello, Mr Boyd. It's George here. The story of the Metrodome ground is being covered by *The Sportz! Magazine* in collaboration with The Ground People; they are planning to revamp the Metrodome grounds,' Mr Elliot said.

'Okay, George. Send me the proposal. I will give you feedback in a couple of days. Meanwhile, tell them to start with interviews and ask them to come up with a convincing story,' Mr Boyd said.

The selected day was a Wednesday. Sophie, Theo and Mr Elliot were waiting for Mr Schultz and Mr Wintringham in the reception of the clubhouse. Both of them arrived in quick succession just before 10 am.

'Good morning gentlemen! Nice to have you aboard,' Mr Elliot said in his professional voice.

'Good morning! Glad to be here,' Mr Schultz said shaking hands with the trio.

'Nice to meet you, folks! Always a pleasure to be at the Metrodome,' Mr Wintringham said warmly.

'Thank you for your time,' Sophie said warmly.

They entered the changing room. An odd smell came out of the room. It was made ready for the interview with all the arrangements in place. Yet, there were signs that the room had been closed down for a long time. There were no corners to the changing rooms. There were benches and wooden lockers for the players to keep their jerseys and kit. And in the center were beds for the injured players. The shower rooms were on the left, and a medical room on the right for the physiotherapy and first-aid. There was a balcony to watch the match from the dressing room and a small kitchen in the back. Sophie tried to visualise how it would have been all those years ago, as now all that was left were mere impressions of benches and lockers on the walls and floors in the room. The beds were long gone, and showers ran dry.

The conversation began and, as said, it was open and none of it was recorded.

'Mr Schultz, what was the one thing that inspired you and your team to go out and play?' Sophie asked.

'I remember the days when I was a coach of the team that traditionally had a great record playing in the varsity games. We always aimed to harness a team spirit. I believed in not conceding a single goal and making the game fun. But more than that, it was the changing room atmosphere that helped the team to perform better. Through banter and pranks, the team gelled together as one unit. And, in such atmosphere players forgot the personal accolades and instead played with one another,' Mr Schultz said.

'Thanks Mr Schultz. Mr Wintringham, I feel honoured to cover the story of this historic stadium. I have become a fan of the Metrodome. Can you tell us, what was your vision when you designed this stadium?' Sophie asked.

'I wanted to provide exceptional sports facilities to the sporting talent at the university. Back then it was just a piece of land with a green field on it. I love sports and played a lot for as long as I could. That inspired me to build this ground and this was my first architectural endeavour,' Mr Wintringham said, remembering the days from the bygone era.

'Tell us something about your philosophy: "You win in the

changing room,"' Sophie said.

'A foundation of a strong team is built in the changing room. Every player as an individual can put in the hard yards, work in the gym and practice. But to go out there as one unit is a different ball game. As a kid, I played football at the varsity games. During one match, the opposite team's coach shook hands with our coach and said, "Finally you have arrived," he paused a bit, then said "... to lose!" with a smirk. I still remember what our coach said: "No! We always come back again and again." That left a lasting impression on my mind. Even today, I believe caring for your team leads you to better places beyond the podium finish.' Mr Wintringham said.

'Thank you, Mr Wintringham. Mr Schultz, tell us something about the changing room speech that you delivered before the big final of the '98 season,' Sophie said.

'It was a nerve-wracking day. Melvin Robinson lead the side and we were up against the Asteroids. It was an El Clasico at the varsity games. The boys were getting ready for the game. I was sitting right there tying my shoelace,' Mr Schultz said pointing his finger towards an empty area. He was narrating the scene with child-like enthusiasm as if it happened yesterday. He continued in his animated way, 'I gathered the team in a huddle and then gave a speech that got the team going when it mattered the most. I still remember the words and they are reverberating in my mind as I sit here.

"If you love the game and think that you have worked hard enough to believe in it; then you were meant to play football and have earned this match! Today is your night, go and play as if your life depended on it. Go, Jaguars, Go!"' Mr Schultz spoke as if he heard the echo within the room.

There was silence for a few minutes in the room. Everyone sat there soaking in the vibes.

'... And the rest of the story is printed in the record books,' Mr Schultz said as a smile played on his lips.

The hour-long conversation went from team spirit in the changing room to building a winning team. Mr Schultz couldn't hold back his emotions as he went back all those years and relived the moments of exhilaration, fun and camaraderie. Mr Wintringham felt nostalgic as he remembered the day when he laid the foundation stone of the stadium.

'I would like to ask a final question to both of you: why do you think the grounds should be revived?' Sophie asked.

'I think the grounds have certain historic importance and heritage. It was built in the year 1972. It had an archaic style of architecture with four stands in the cardinal directions and a pavilion at the centre just beside the grounds. The changing rooms were constructed as part of the pavilion. The brown coloured roof and the steps for the spectators were a classic example of a stadium from a bygone era. Such grounds are fast disappearing and I feel they should be around so that posterity can learn about the sports culture from the past, not just from textbooks, but by seeing and experiencing the facilities in the real world,' Mr Wintringham said.

'I think we must revive this stadium because it has seen large crowds of students and spectators gathered to support their teams at the games. The players that played during those years always played their hearts out and practised as if there was no tomorrow! If anything, it would help the students get inspired to join the sport for their well-being,' Mr Schultz said.

A picture was shot with Mr Schultz and Mr Wintringham. Sophie gave both of them a souvenir.

'Good luck with your endeavour!' both said in unison as they took their leave.

Sophie came back to the office. She thanked Theo and Mr Elliot, then started writing down the story of the stadium. It was published in *The Sportz! Magazine* the following month. The story made the right noise on social media and TV. The buzz around it reached Mr Boyd. It made him ponder over Mr Elliot's proposal which he had read and kept aside. A committee decided to revive the Metrodome. The Ground People started working as they joined hands with none other than Mr Edward Wintringham.

In the days that followed, Sophie and Theo covered stories of more such grounds around the country and later published a book called *The Soccer Days*.

The Shut Door

Leelarai Weesakul

The lies you told us, the unreachable dream,
Work hard you say as we stumble through the seams,
Unseen and unheard, with nowhere left to go,
Our words left unspoken, a generation of shut doors.

Give us space, give us room, give us air and let us breathe,
We suffocate through this life, a baggage left from your greed.
You were the screw ups, we know that you are,
Yet we bear your weight, your sins and your scars.

Be grateful to your parents, be grateful to your chains.
For you bear their burdens, their rooms left unchanged.
A relic of the past yet we suffer through it all,
The fossil has spoken yet it is us who will fall.

The dust will collect, the mold and rot inside,
A system that festers, a room to bury alive.
We want to move on, burn it all and start again,
But where will we turn to? There's no room for us to win.

Ode to Paper

Sarah Ushurhe

Your origin stemmed from various fibres
Later the pith of the plant used by ancients
To record their history
Your life was cut short as a tree
But reborn into paper for us to use
Helping to manifest our forms of creativity
And providing us with the news
Your weight and purpose varies
As does my collection
Such joy from using you all the time
You know our deepest, darkest thoughts
I fold, slice, stick and cut into you
And still, you withstand it all
Bound together stories are told
Bound together I can create my own
You lie still, waiting for your purpose
That has yet to be set
Until my fingers touch you

Part II

General Submissions

Biscuit

Ellen Dorrington

Biscuit is lost. Biscuit is our cat. He can't ask for help, because he can't talk. He *can* talk, I think, we just can't understand what he says. *Meow Meow Meow*, Biscuit says. *My name is Biscuit. I live on 44 Spruce Street.*

I'm looking for Biscuit. I haven't ever been on this road by myself before, but I was playing in the garden, and I saw a flash of orange, just like Biscuit. He is the colour of a ginger nut and his fur is soft and he is fast. I chased after him, and now I am on a different road.

I'm going to ask that old lady for help. She's standing right by the traffic lights, peering at the button for the green man. I am good at waiting for the green man, and I'll tell you a secret: if you look at the bottom of the button a special knob spins round and round, and you can't see it, only if you're little like me and know where to look. Mummy says the secret button is for blind people, and I also know that it is for spies.

The old lady is too close to the cars. When I get to her, I can feel the big metal whirring of them speeding past, roaring like dragons. I tug on the bottom of her t-shirt. She doesn't look at me.

Her t-shirt is grass-coloured with little pearls embroidered on it. There's a big soup stain on her chest, like a splodge, to let her know where her heart is.

'Hello!' I say. Still no answer. 'Hello?'

Maybe she is deaf. There is a boy in my class who is deaf and I know how to say good morning and one song, "Kookaburra", all in sign language.

I do a sign for the old lady but she doesn't pay attention. I jump three times.

'Hello! Hello! Hello!' I say with each jump.

Only then does she fix her little eyes on me. They are bright blue, watery blue, and too shiny for my liking. It looks like crying eyes. Maybe I shouldn't ask her for help.

But she smiles. She has very few teeth. They are far apart from each other and they are yellow. This old lady needs to clean her teeth, like how I do, for two whole long minutes, and my toothbrush plays a song to tell me when to stop. The music makes it not so bad. I do a dance in the bathroom until my big brother Andrew tells me to stop.

'Hello,' the old lady says, looking down at me. Her voice is rough like sandpaper. It sounds as if she hasn't spoken for a long time, like her voice has been strangled out of her. Maybe she has a cold, even though it's summer, and nobody gets a cold in the summer.

'I'm looking for my cat,' I say. Talking to her now makes my tummy hurt. The old lady is shuffling away from the road. Her back is curved like a giant letter C and she plods one foot in front of the other. She moves like a tortoise, and comes to stand in front of me.

I want to go back home and to my mummy but I need to find Biscuit. Biscuit can only meow and he doesn't have pockets so he doesn't have any money.

'I'm looking for Eileen,' the old lady tells me. She peers at me very closely, like I might be hiding Eileen somewhere.

'Is that your cat?' I ask her. She laughs, but as soon as she makes one chuckle she starts coughing. She wobbles as she coughs, and the cough comes from deep inside her lungs, like something bad bad is there. It is rattling around inside her. The old lady coughs for ages before she stops and when she does she is puff puff puffing. Her breath is rasping, which is a new word I learnt in school, and Mrs Woods gave me a sticker for using it in a sentence.

The old lady is rasping.

'Do you need a doctor?' I ask her, and then my insides feel all twisty, and I say, 'Are you going to die?'

'Me? No!' the old lady says, still puffing. She puts her hand on the green man box to steady herself, and I watch her to make sure she does not fall.

'I'm too young to die,' the old lady says. A pause. 'I'm looking for Eileen.'

'I'm looking for my cat.'

'Maybe they are together,' the old lady says, 'maybe Eileen has your cat.'

'Maybe!' I am excited. I think Eileen might be another old lady, and Biscuit likes old ladies. When my Nana came to visit from Jamaica, Biscuit jumped in her lap and she yelled and pushed him off. My Nana does not like cats but once I saw her, in secret, stroking Biscuit on the very top of his head, where he likes it most. He started purring like a cat robot. I saw his bright orange hairs all over Nana's black skirt.

You can collect these things when you're a spy. They're called clues, and it helps you work out what is true. Sometimes grown-ups lie and it's a spy's job to work out why.

'I think Eileen has gone to the seaside,' the old lady says, 'she liked it there.'

The seaside seems very far away. We went there last summer for our holiday, and the car ride was long and made me sleepy. Biscuit wouldn't be at the seaside because he doesn't like water and I'm not allowed to put him in the bath, only Mummy is allowed to wash him, and when she does I hear her shouting "bloody cat!" which is a swearword and I'm not allowed to say it.

'I don't think Biscuit is at the seaside,' I say to the old lady, but she is not listening. She is humming a song to herself, and I think it is the one we had to sing in assembly, *Oh I do like to be beside the seaside.* But I could be wrong. Spies sometimes are wrong.

'Eileen liked the seaside. It's where she met Albert,' the old lady says, and she opens her eyes and looks at me, urgently. 'Where's Albert?'

Who's Albert? It is becoming hard to keep track of who is missing.

'We'll find Albert after we find Biscuit and Eileen,' I say to the old lady, and she smiles, all of her fear gone. It looks like she has melted. I think she needs to sit down.

My Nana needs to sit down after she has played with me. But it's okay, because normally she gives me a cuddle. Even though she is an old lady, she is not like this old lady, who is as white as a cloud. My Nana is sturdy. I told her this, and she laughed, and said, 'Nonsense. I am just fat.'

Why am I thinking about Nana when Biscuit is lost? My thoughts are all jumbly. I imagine them like strings and I pull them together in one big knot. Biscuit is lost. Biscuit is our cat.

'Do you know how to get to Eileen?' I ask the old lady.

'Yes!'

This old lady has a voice that wobbles when she is excited. My Nana has a booming voice, it can be scary when she shouts, but she also laughs more than anyone else and tells me I am the most beautiful girl in the world. This old lady smiles only a few times and it is a rain type of smile. When you try to make the best of things but you wish it was sun sunny instead.

I wish my Nana wasn't so far away because even though she hates Biscuit she would help me find him.

'It's this way,' the old lady says. She reaches out to grip my arm, her fingers cold and knobbly. They grasp me tightly, and I feel the old lady's weight, too heavy. She is hurting me.

She pulls me forward, down the street towards the high street and all the shops, including the corner shop that always has a dog tied up outside it, which is cruel, because the dog should be allowed to come inside.

We walk along for a few steps. The old lady walks too slowly, but at least we are not near the cars anymore. I am starting to get annoyed. I try to uncurl her fingers from my arm one by one, but as soon as I get one off and work on the other, she's touching me again.

'Please let go of me,' I say to her, but she shakes her head.

'You're taking me to Eileen.'

'No!' I don't know where I am going beyond the shops. I try to line up the roads in my head and make them into patterns, but I have forgotten where to go. What if I forget my way home? What if I am lost like Biscuit?

'I need to go home,' I say.

The old lady stops. She sighs, and when she looks at me, she is angry. 'You're useless. Why aren't we going to Eileen?'

Her words feel like little bee stings, but on the inside, in my chest.

Nana never says things like this to me. On the phone, just yesterday, I told her I had lost Biscuit. She said it is okay, he knows the way home because last time she visited me she put butter on his paws, and that helps him find his way back. I asked her when she was coming to visit me and she said not this year.

Mummy took the phone away from me. She had watery eyes, like the old lady.

Into the phone she said, 'I know, I know. I'll do it — maybe when the cat comes back. It'll be too hard otherwise.'

What is too hard?

I do not know where I am. The shops do not look like the shops I visit with my mummy after school. The old lady is still holding me and I don't know how to make her let me go, how to find Eileen, or where Biscuit is, or who Albert is, or how to get home.

I want to cry. I feel the hotness rising, feel water in my eyes.

If I blink there will be tears but I am a brave girl.

I was worried about Biscuit but now I am worried about the old lady too.

'I don't know where Eileen is,' I say to the old lady. I know she doesn't have a mummy but I don't know why. My Nana doesn't have a mummy or a daddy or a husband. She lives with my uncle, in Jamaica.

Last month Mummy went to Jamaica and she didn't take anyone with her. When you are a spy you look for clues, even when you don't want to. Even when they make you feel heavy, like when you want to take off your coat to go and play.

'You should go home,' I say to the old lady, 'Eileen might be at home.'

The old lady nods but she does not move. I wait and it feels like a whole minute goes past before she speaks again. She says, 'Hello. Can you help me find Eileen?'

I start to cry. I don't know what to do. Everyone walks past us, looking at us a little funnily, like we are a big dog poo in the street.

I find it hard to breathe. I think what I'm doing now is wailing, noisy, and it makes me feel like a siren. A woman finally stops and bends down, shopping bags in her hands. They clatter to the floor.

'Hello, love,' she says, 'do you and your gran need help?'

I don't know how to tell her about everything that is wrong. I cry louder, making little gulpy breaths I don't know how to stop.

There is a police man now. He is holding the old lady's shoulder and talking to her, his voice making a shushing sound. He has his special hat on, with a shiny silver badge, so everyone knows he is a policeman. People turn and look at him, at us, because when a policeman is there, it usually means there is trouble.

We are in trouble. We are the trouble.

'Eileen,' he says, his round face bright and pale. It reminds me of the moon. 'We're glad we found you, Eileen.'

Hope

Rahama Hassan

Lately, it feels as though the world is falling apart

Like the Earth is an old woolly hat

Being pulled at

By its loose threads

But tonight, the universe is dreamy

So, I grab a pen, open my notebook

And start to sew —

The Little Cheese Shop

Rebecca White

Where the Saône river winds through Burgundy, there is a bend in the river at the ancient town of Mâcon. At this bend there is a narrow lane that winds north between tall eighteenth century buildings that crowd in on one another. Down this lane, where the sunlight shines through a gap in the buildings, sat a small, inconsequential cheese shop.

Above the shop lived three generations of women; Esmé the owner, old at thirty-five, her elderly mother and teenage daughter, Amalie. The street door to the workroom of the cheese shop was wide open on this warm morning and just inside stood Esmé, one hand on her hip, the other holding a bottle of rat poison.

'There was another one this morning. This one was huge,' she called to Grand-mère, who was setting out the cheese for the day in the shop-front.

'Ah, they are a fact of life my dear. Everyone needs to eat.'

'This should take care of it.' Esmé set out the poison and put the bottle on the worktop in the utility area of the workroom. 'They are a pest!' she shouted through to Grand-mère. 'Parasites living off whatever they can take from us.'

The soothing strains of violins and music broke the peace;
Amalie had turned the radio on in the little flat above the shop.
Through the floorboards, Esmé could hear her daughter singing
along to the gentle harmonies of the Everly Brothers' "Let It Be
Me".

'Argh, that girl!' Esmé went to the small wooden staircase at
the back of the workroom that led to the compact, but homely,
flat. She crossed herself as she passed the picture of Our Lady
hanging askew in the dark stairwell and called up, 'Amalie,
switch that music off, it's time for school now!' Not that Esmé
minded pop music, but it reminded her that her own youth had
been ripped away from her. The radio went silent and there was
Amalie, bouncing down the stairs with all the vigour of her
sixteen years, satchel in hand, ready for school. Esmé caught
her breath every time she looked at her child. Her long blonde
hair backcombed like her movie idol, Brigitte Bardot, and her
fashionable short skirt showed an excessive amount of the
young girl's legs for Esmé's liking.

'What's with the eye make-up, I've told you I don't like you
looking older than you are.' Esmé knew she sounded like her
own mother when she said things like that.

Amalie answered with her customary good-natured light
heart, 'It's just like Frankie's, and you said you liked hers.'

Esmé softened, remembering the feeling of wanting to be
grown up and replied, warmly, 'But she's not my daughter.'
Esmé gazed into Amalie's innocent aquamarine eyes for a
second and wondered for the umpteenth time if her only child
had inherited any of her own qualities. Then Amalie kissed her
Maman on the cheek and called to the front of the shop, 'Au
revoir Grand-mère,' before whizzing out of the back door.

'I must talk to Amalie when she gets home from school
about not leaving the bin out,' Esmé said to Grand-mère as she

joined her to open the shop for the morning.

'The poor child, you cannot blame her. We must make sure everything is secure, not her.'

'Can't be too vigilant.' With that, Esmé fetched more greaseproof paper to wrap purchased cheese in, as Grand-mère served their first customer of the day.

It was the turn of the day, when the heat was retreating and shadows began to crawl their way along the deep lanes. Amalie was home from school having been to L'Alchimie's for milk shakes with her friends on the way back. She now hung around the shop humming her favourite pop song, hoping she'd be allowed to meet more of her friends later. Grand-mère was out shopping for dinner and Esmé was busy cleaning up in the back room of the shop. Standing up, she put her worn hands on her back and stretched, catching her reflection in the glass of the door. Wisps of dark hair had escaped from her thin ponytail and were hanging around her face. The muted glass was kind to her reflection but she knew her face was lined with the cares of rebuilding a life, a town and a country after the ravages of war. She smoothed her apron down over the creases in her faded skirt, not something she could ever see her modern young daughter wearing.

The bell for the shop door rang. 'I'll go,' trilled Amalie and off she jaunted into the front to serve the customer. It was a well-dressed middle aged man. His tailored suit was of a fine cotton, the type of cloth ideal for this weather. He had sharp features and short, clipped hair that Amalie noticed when he tipped his trilby to say a polite hello. 'How can I help you today?' she asked brightly.

'What would you recommend I have with my dinner tonight?' he replied. His tone was polite but with a hint of an accent that Amalie could not quite place.

'Well sir, that all depends on what you are eating,' she answered playfully.

'You are quite right,' he replied with courtesy. 'The butcher down the road sold me a steak and I have a bottle of your finest local burgundy, so now all I need is some lovely local cheese to finish my meal. Could you recommend something?'

'Well, if you really want a local cheese, you should try Mâconnais. It is in the blue family of cheeses, but the blue is on the rind not the centre, which is a lovely creamy colour. It has a salty, tangy flavour, and melts in your mouth when you eat it.' Amalie was getting into her subject now. 'It's my favourite but we've sold out today as it's quite popular around here.'

'That is a pity, you have given me an appetite for it.'

'We get some every day from a local farm so I could put some aside for you tomorrow.'

'Then I shall have to come back tomorrow to try it.'

'You are passing through our town?'

'Yes, I lived here for a while a long time ago and wanted to come back. Many things have changed.'

'Ah, I hope you are enjoying your stay here.'

'It gets better and better all the time.'

'Bon! Well, we have other cheeses that will go better with your wine tonight. You have the Mâcon burgundy, oui?'

'Ja, I have the red to complement the steak.'

Amalie had grown up around wine and cheese — living in the Bourgogne region it goes with the territory — but she suddenly felt out of her depth. 'I believe a good cheese to go with that is this one,' she pointed towards one with a soft, white rind. 'Excuse me, I will just check.' Amalie went to the door that lies between the shop front and the workroom at the back and called, 'Maman, the Brillat-Savarin goes well with a red burgundy, oui?'

Esmé was busy mopping the floor.

'Er,' she called back. Being a touch distracted, she had to get her thoughts onto wine and cheese instead of mops and buckets. 'Oui, ma petite, it will go well with that,' she replied, a little out of breath from the effort of ferocious sponging.

'Maman, are you okay?'

'Oui, chérie!'

Amalie smiled at the amiable gentleman and turned back to the cheese. 'Ah, so, the Brillat-Savarin is also from Bourgogne, although not specifically Mâcon. It is extremely creamy and rich yet delicate with a light, sour flavour to balance the creaminess. As you see the rind is very white and dewy; it is supposed to give the appearance of snow.'

'I am incredibly impressed; you know so much about cheese.'

'Ah, well, um, it is written on the back of the card there.' Amalie pointed to the cards giving the names and prices of the cheese and felt a modicum of guilt for cheating a little. But, he was right, she knew her cheeses.

The gentleman laughed, a sweet and sincere laugh. 'You astonish me, you have such knowledge for one so young. Tell me, did your father teach you all this?'

'Non, I have never met my father. My mother owns the shop and taught me everything I know.'

'She must be a very intelligent lady.'

'She is.'

'Now, I must ask you about one more cheese. Tell me about the Munster here.'

'Ah, that is from a region north of here, near the Vosges mountains and the Rhine.'

The gentleman nodded in acknowledgement, 'That is why it sounds so familiar.'

'It has a smooth and slightly sticky texture and a savoury, tangy taste. As you see, the rind looks a bit wrinkly. It is what we call "washed". It has a red coating to begin with but with repeated washings it becomes quite, um, humid. It is that which gives the cheese its aroma and texture. The rind, you see, protects the cheese but also builds the complex flavour.'

'I am so impressed with you and your knowledge. May I ask,

what is your name?'

'My name? I am Amalie.'

'It is a pleasure to meet you, Amalie.'

'Thank you. Would you like to try the cheese?'

'Ja, I would like both the Munster and the snow cheese, s'il vous plaît. And I will come back tomorrow to try your Mâcon…'

'Oui, Mâconnais.' She chuckled at his effort to pronounce the French word.

'Mâconnais,' he repeated softly, savouring each syllable.

While Amalie cut, wrapped and sold the gentleman the cheeses, they had no idea their conversation was being watched. Behind the door, peering through the hinge gap where the door met the doorframe, stood Esmé, breathless.

Grand-mère picked her way along the cobbles down the little narrow lane towards the shop. The disappearing sun cast long shadows against the coarse walls and ancient wooden shutters on the houses. Grand-mère felt the heaviness of her basket full of food for dinner, comprising unsold produce from the grocers and butchers. Grand-mère was nearly at the shop entrance when she saw a man exit. A striking, tall man dressed in a tailored suit. As he neared her, he raised his trilby politely and she noticed his clipped fair hair coupled with his pale skin. His aquamarine eyes fixed on her for a moment before he sauntered on. Grand-mère flattened herself against the wall of the closest house. Her free hand grasped the rough plaster for support. Her chest ached with the shortening of her breath and all she could hear was the pumping of blood in her temples. She stared after him, unable to move. Her free hand moved to support her heart from thumping out of her chest. It couldn't be. It was unmistakeable. She was staring down the lane after a man whom she vowed she would never forget, ever. She was staring after the SS Nazi officer who determined their destiny.

Her Turn

Deirdre Maher

His tongue
tip to clit.

Cunning

oh
so delicate!

Deep and sweet
and soft and strong
thrilling chords in unison
taste my essence sip and savour
instrument of purest pleasure
reaching exquisite crescendo!

notes receding…

still
the
echo

lingers

in

the
core
of

me.

THE WAVES HAVE COME

Esther Reynolds

We were supposed to meet Signe at the apartment for the handover of keys, but instead we met Lucas, her boyfriend. He was friendly enough and took an immediate liking to Dana, eyeing her like a predator proudly looks over its kill. He didn't look at me once, the old, worn out beta. But Dana, in her usual, nonchalant way, smiled at me, flicked her hair back and took no notice of his attentions. That always comforted me immensely. She knew that Lucas was being overly friendly, perhaps to make himself more appealing than he usually was, but she was having none of it. She never did. She was mine, completely and utterly.

I still wish Signe had been there to meet us.

He showed us round the tiny, one-bed apartment, explained where to leave the keys when we were done and left, a docile expression of a man ignored.

Then there was just us; a week in Copenhagen all to ourselves.

The sun streamed through the window-doors, illuminating the simplistic, Scandinavian living room. It was a room from an Ikea catalogue; sparse, utilitarian, white furnishings, nothing more than what was required, nothing that would keep you inside for any length of time.

A scattering of tourist leaflets were laid out on the table; I noted to have a look at them later. We still hadn't decided how we would spend the week. Dana stood barefoot on the hardwood floors, toes soaking up the warmth. The floorboards groaned as I moved to stand next to her in my scruffy airplane trainers and looked out onto the apartments in the block opposite us.

'We'll have carpets when we live together,' I said.

Dana nodded.

I glanced sideways at her. She didn't look at me.

'Let's see what's in the kitchen,' she suggested and swept out of the room all in one. I followed, a docile expression of a man ignored.

We spent the evening browsing the leaflets and searching for places to go on my iPad. We planned, checked the weather, adjusted the plan accordingly, and went to bed.

Our first day consisted of visiting castles and old places, exploring the centre of town, ducking in and out of cafés as the rain came and went, vowing to be better prepared tomorrow. Dana was ebullient. She picked out the café for our lunch, she took nearly three hundred photos of the architecture, the museum exhibits, the history, the culture. She seemed more relaxed than I'd ever seen her in my seven-and-a-half-months of knowing her. We were living in London at the time; but according to her, it was not the same as this city, not at all.

I was largely underwhelmed. Why did we have to travel all the way to Denmark to see these palaces? London had one of the most famous palaces in the world and it was only six tube stops away from my flat.

She barely looked at me the entire day. Only at lunch and dinner, when we were forced into a tiny wooden booth or crammed around a glass table under an umbrella, was she obliged to look at me. Of course, this was after she'd joked with the waiter, shown me all the photos she'd taken that afternoon, flicked through the leaflets in her bag, checked her emails and rummaged through her bag again to find lip balm. It was only after all this did her eyes finally meet mine and we exchanged small talk. Apart from that, her eyes and heart belonged to the city.

We ended the evening early, agreeing to head back to the apartment as the cold was becoming unbearable.

'More layers tomorrow,' I muttered on the train back.

Dana nodded once, curtly.

Back at the apartment, her attention turned to the kitchen. We'd popped into a supermarket on the way back and we'd spent our spare krone on some snacks and drinks for the evening. She made the dinner, decided which crisps we should graze on first.

She came back into the living room with the drinks. Switched on the TV. Found a suitable Danish channel to watch. Found the subtitles. Then turned the subtitles off because they were "too distracting".

I found I had been counting the hours and minutes since she last asked me a question.

The next morning, she was up before me.

I hadn't realised she was awake until I woke, groggily flinging out a hand to feel her in bed, my hand landing on a rumpled pillow instead. I didn't move for a while, fighting off sleep. When I finally dragged myself out of bed, I found her sitting comfortably in a chair next to the window, looking down on the street below. Coffee in hand, blanket half draped around her, she looked like a photograph from a travel magazine.

'You're up early,' I commented.

She smiled, but didn't turn around. Sipped her coffee, shifted the book on her lap that I hadn't noticed.

'Just couldn't get back to sleep,' she said softly. I sank into the sofa.

'What are you reading?'

She showed me the cover.

'"Seven Gothic Tales,"' I read aloud, haltingly. 'Any good?'

She shrugged. 'Maybe I haven't acquired a Danish taste in books yet.'

I know she meant it as a joke — she smiled at me — but I didn't react. I didn't want her to have a Danish taste in books. I wanted her to have her taste in books; romantic, silly, crammed with cringey innuendos and clichés and the most dramatic, unlikely storylines, the kind you pick up in an airport for two-ninety-nine. Her apartment back in London was filled with those sorts of books.

That afternoon found us sat in a light, airy bakery in Frederiksberg, pastries in hand, coffees steaming on the table, too hot to sip. We'd travelled for over half an hour on the subway — albeit we'd taken a train two stops too far and had to backtrack — and I wasn't sure we were still in the city, but Dana maintained that we were.

We wandered through the Sondermarken, the air chill and fresh. The park was depressingly plain and bare. This didn't seem to matter to Dana. She had her camera out, picture after picture. I suggested a selfie with the park rolling away behind us. She dutifully agreed and we took the picture on my phone; the first and only one. I hadn't found much else particularly worth a place in the limited memory of my phone.

When I looked back at it that evening, Dana wasn't looking at the camera and she wasn't smiling. Her lips were pursed and her eyes were far away.

It was late afternoon on Thursday when I saw that look again. We'd returned to the rental briefly so I could wash and we could both get ready to go out for dinner.

I stumbled out of the shower, blinking water and soap out of my eyes. I grumbled something to Dana about the stinging sensation, towelling my hair dry and wandering into the lounge.

She stood with one foot crossed over the other, hands hanging at her side, that faraway look focused on an un-hung print that had been stored behind the sofa. She'd pulled it out and was now studying it, warming her feet on the wood floor. I stopped, a little worried I'd frighten her by pulling her out of the reverie. She swayed a little. I glanced at the print. To me, it was nude coloured shapes on a nude background. Nothing particularly notable, but she seemed taken with it.

I slipped away into the bedroom to finish getting ready.

She didn't mention the painting, or her thoughtful trance at dinner. She chattered on, drew the waiter into a fairly long conversation about pastries, and their Danish history, showed me some more photos and then brought up an article she'd read about how the Danes are the happiest in Europe. I listened, nodded, struggled with whether to bring up the painting.

What would I even say? Did you like the painting? Would you want something similar in the living room when we move in together? It all sounded so weak and inconsequential.

'This food is amazing,' Dana muttered over her dinner. 'Why don't we have food like this back home?'

I knew it was a rhetorical question, but I paused eating to search for an answer. I didn't have one.

What were you thinking about when you were looking at the painting?

'Do you want dessert? I could definitely have dessert. I want to see if they have... I can't remember what it's called. It's like cream with cookies and berries and other things. But it's more than that. Oh, I can't remember. I'll know it if I see it. I want to try that if they have it.'

She had to settle for something called Danish Dream Cake, of which I had a couple of small bites. It was rather nice, though I didn't admit it.

Why that painting? What is it about it? What got you so focused on it?

In the end, I never mentioned the painting. We returned to

the apartment and I flicked through the leaflets, sorting them into a pile of sights we'd seen and sights we hadn't. Dana switched on the TV and ignored me.

It was our last day. I woke to Dana missing from the bed again. She was in the armchair, in the weak morning sunlight, reading "Seven Gothic Tales" again. I hated that book. It was so far removed from anything she usually liked.

'Sleep well?'

Dana nodded but didn't look up. I scooped up the leaflets of sights we hadn't seen from the coffee table.

'I thought we could take a trip to Tivoli today, and then to the Glyptoteket. They're close together. There's lockers at the train station we can leave our bags in.'

Lucas crossed my mind briefly. We'd have to check out in a couple of hours and I wondered if he'd be around. Or whether we'd finally meet Signe.

'Dana?'

She finally looked up. 'Yes, that sounds good.' Deadpan. Didn't hear a word I said.

I finished getting ready and packing up, while Dana fixed us breakfast. I was sat on the sofa flicking through the Tivoli leaflet, looking at entrance fees, when she came back into the living room with two bowls of muesli... and stopped.

I looked up. She had that look in her eyes again, faraway, thoughtful. She wasn't even on this planet.

'Dana?' I asked quietly.

She turned to me.

'I've decided to stay.'

I blinked a couple of times, trying to process.

'What? Where?' I asked stupidly.

'Here,' she said brightly. 'I'm staying here.'

'You - you can't. We only have the room for today. Our flight is tonight.'

She set the bowls down on the table.

'I'll get a room elsewhere. Just for a few days. Until I find my feet.'

'I don't understand,' I mumbled, although I was definitely scared of understanding. This was the most eye contact she'd given me in five days and I was relishing it.

'I'm staying here. I don't want to go back home. Lots of people speak English here, I have a degree. It shouldn't be too hard to find a job.' She shrugged. 'I'm staying.'

'Indefinitely?' She nodded. 'Wh-what about us?'

'We'll find other people. We'll move on.' Her voice turned cold and it felt as though she had shut a door on me. I just stared at her for what felt like an aeon; she took it, held my gaze. I never wanted to leave her eyes. I wanted to remember them, because this was going to be the last chance I had. I knew then that I'd lost her. She was already gone. She'd picked out another apartment, had sent out her CV to a couple of companies, had planned how she was going to acquire a bike and cycle everywhere.

I let out the breath I'd been holding.

'We still have today though. Let's go to Tivoli and the Glypto... place.'

It felt unbelievably strange to be sightseeing in a foreign city with a woman I loved, with the knowledge that she would leave me at about twenty minutes past five when I would catch a train to the airport. I walked around in dumb silence. I couldn't even gather the energy to make a trivial comment in a weak attempt at conversation.

Dana, on the other hand, walked with me in happy oblivion. She seemed unaware of my conflicted state. A large part of me wanted to walk away from her right then and there, catch a train and sit in the airport alone for the remainder of the day. I wanted space to be miserable, but I couldn't be miserable while Dana was trying so hard to act as if we were a couple enjoying the last day of our first holiday together. She took picture after picture, lingering over the marble statues in the Glyptoteket.

To be fair to the Danes, it was a striking building. And one I'm sure

I would have appreciated, had it been in more usual circumstances.

We passed through arched halls of artefacts and statues, through a large mosaiced courtyard with more marble figurines occupying each pillar. I found it eerie. Their life-likeness was striking, and a little disconcerting. I tried to look into the eyes of a marble woman wrapped from head to toe in a robe, striding purposefully. But her face was cast down and I couldn't quite see her clearly; like Dana, this alabaster woman seemed to be avoiding my gaze.

We stopped for a coffee. She showed me a couple of her photos and I nodded at them numbly. She sat back in her seat, crossed her legs and flicked through her phone. I stared at her while she did this, but she didn't notice me. I took the opportunity to commit her face to memory; her dark curls, startlingly bright eyes. Her skin was pale and milky like the marble, veins of pale blue showing through at her forehead.

In the end, she accompanied me to the airport, seeing as she'd already bought the ticket. I handed her the remainder of my krone at security.

'I will make this easy for you,' she said quietly, the first sign she was feeling any sadness at this. 'Goodbye.' Her last word to me was quick and I almost didn't catch it as she turned and walked off.

I felt something in my chest cave in on itself. That was it. That was that. That was... over.

It was simultaneously the strangest and most painful breakup I have ever been a part of, and a sharp, sudden sickness in my gut made me turn heel. I needed more than anything to be away from this place, especially that spot three, now five feet away where she had left me. Now twenty feet. Oh fuck. I needed more than the half mile to my gate. I needed five hundred and ninety-four. Perhaps that would be enough.

Lie

Millie Turner

'Here, lie',

They told me,

Offering a space before them,

Where I could lay,

And be a body,

For their uses and misuses,

Skin and bone and flesh and abuses,

So that I'd be less dented knuckle and more soft petal,

But me,

Just being a body that they could fill with their empty space,

It turns out *nothing* turns to poison when it's ignored for too long and so now,

Here lies,

The body that used to be mine,

She looks softer,

Rounder, like both petal and knuckle but now,

As I roll the bends of my arms and fingers before the gleaming eyes of a bulb,

Casting coal projections onto walls too weak to be scrubbed,

I see that,

Soft petal was the pseudonym to the knuckles you knew wouldn't graze you,

Soft petal was the pseudonym to my weakness,

Because I loved you,

And you knew that when you peeled away the plaster,

And knit me a sweater of asbestos,

I'd love so hard it'd kill me.

Where I Read

Molly Hills

The winter to some may mark the end of outdoor activity in my latitude, but to me it marks the beginning. To wrap up warm, with a fleece and a scarf. To leave the house with a tangerine in the pocket and a flask of tea in the hand. To walk along the river, to find my reading spot unoccupied; and sit comfortably for the first time after a heaving summer, is to feel most alive. Most invigorated. Finally, I can breathe properly and feel the air on my face without it prickling my skin like tiny flies that persistently reappear after every slap. No sweaty slick slides down my back. No hoards of humans elbowing for space. The world and I both exhale a happy sigh. Winter has come at last.

There's a little spot by the river, walking up the Portsmouth road from Thames Ditton to Kingston, where I like to go and read. There are many little spots along this stretch. In fact, the entire boardwalk is made specifically for those of us in search for a place they can call their little spot. It's not the greatest, most central part of London, but there's ample seating, seemingly zero supervision, and a magnificent array of sights and smells, organic and affirming. We each get to have a little spot. To watch, to read, to write or to chat. It's abundant and it's free.

There is ample seating on this stretch of the river. Accommodating a wide spectrum of preferred seating situations. Dozens of benches snake along the dense hedgerow that blocks the boardwalk from the snores of the main road, each bench with a plaque dedicated to someone loved and lost. They dutifully support their occupants with ancestral nobility. To sit on a named bench is to feel like a child sitting on a grandparent's lap. There's a kindness to it, like they are sharing their spot with you. They say things like: "To Joan, who loved this river like a best friend" and "There's nothing I'd rather do, than sit right here with you". I like to sit on Joan's bench. I like to think she met her love on this very stretch of the Thames. A drink too many at the Fox and Hound before stumbling home holding hands, depositing themselves on a bench for a clumsy kiss before a silly conversation about geese. I do like to sit on Joan's bench, but it's not where I read.

Across the walkway from the benches, a grassy bank slopes towards the river. A handsome spot for the young university student to roll up a cigarette and recline with a book in the sun, shading the glare from their face. People like to sit in little clusters here. One will dangle their legs in the river, dipping in and out of the cluster's meandering conversation. The other plays music on their speaker. Lounging, laughing. Nonchalant.

Further up the boardwalk the bank has a paved section with railings that run between the path and the river. A toddler in a navy duffle coat and wellies throws bread down for the swans with dad. The ducks squabble over the crumbs. The geese laugh along with the toddler.

The people-watching here is divine, if people-watching is what you enjoy. The gentle social engineering of the seating arrangements allow for a unique opportunity for engagement. The wooden amphitheatre style seating further up the river encourages a shared seating culture for casual conversations with strangers. Whereas the benches are a few feet apart from each other, for those who wish to sit alone but within grazing distance of another human.

Just past the railings there's a small cafe. The cafe doesn't appear to have a name and pours fair coffee at a fair price. But there is a small cafe. Here, people sit under the three modest maples that stand to attention in even the most violent of weather. Their employment on this riverside is guard-like, much like the poplars on the other side. You can sit beneath them in the heat of the day or the torment of a storm. They never seem to fluster. They never seem to mind.

My cat-like obsession to find the perfect spot leads me to the bench of "Gladys and Bill. 1909 – 1986. Forever in our hearts." It stands about twenty feet from the cafe and marks the beginning of the line of benches. There is a wide-beamed barge moored opposite which often has a boxer dog lounging on a mattress on the deck. Every bench faces the south, meaning you get the sun on your face for the most gilded hours of the day. It's when I'm sat on this borrowed bench that I have the most pleasant, most fruitful hours of the day. I can write like a demon, with fervent concentration that comes to me as easily as if I were in a vacuum. The soft sounds of life are gentle enough not to steal my focus, but still beat on with pulse. A battery that charges my momentum onward. I look up only from time to time, and just for a second. I cast my eyes to the dog on the mattress, the three lovely maples, the magnificent line of poplars and the toddler, before closing my eyes and returning to work. I read like I'm eating pasta, I breathe like the air smells of linen.

I don't get much time with this spot. I suppose that is what makes it so special. One of the unchanging truths of human nature is our attraction to unavailability. In winter, we long for the sight of tennis balls sailing through blue skies, bare feet in the grass. In summer, we just want to breathe. In the three short months of autumn, I find the hourglass runs faster. The lead up to Christmas begins and I stave it off like the ending of a good book, feeling how many pages I have left with gritted teeth, instead of enjoying and savouring the words I have left. The best kind of glory is the fleeting kind. The intangible moments that can only be enjoyed by our presence. To both soak them in, and soak in them from a spot we can call our own. Thank you Gladys and Bill for this one, I promise to make the most of it.

The Gutter Crow

Morgan Bratli

Mad, I must be! The thick dark of the night must be warping my perception, for it is more acute than the senses of any old man living! It is nothing; the wind up the chimney, the groaning of a settling building. It is nothing; nothing, I say. Why, then, do the hellish sounds never cease? Noises, oh those wretched noises from across the room. My eyes seek sleep, scour every corner for it. I know it hides somewhere in the dark, but I cannot find it. Rattling, creaking, louder and louder the sounds grow; gradually, a din building to a clamour. My eyes may be wide but there exists no light. If I open the shutters sleeping lids, I will be robbed! I want no robbers; damn them, damn them for stealing away my light. Thieves all, degenerates all! It must be nothing! I know it must be nothing. I am not mad, I am not! It must be simply a scurrying rat or an excited crow taking leap from the gutter to find prey.

But my ears — the vile terror which came unto them; creaking and breathing, paralysing my bones and forcing my chest to swell at faster a pace. I hear, I feel, a shadowy presence in the dense dark. Their hideous wide eye is upon mine. Without thought I spring up, my naked feet touching the cold floor. I do not rise, I cannot.

'Who's there?' I speak into the impenetrable dark, no voice giving answer. Nothing at all but for the frenzied pounding of my heart reverberating within my skull. Here I sit for an eternity, here on the very edge of my bed with sharpened ears that hearken not a sound, not a single chirp of a bird or a drunken yell from the streets. Who could do this hell to me? I have wronged no man ever in my life! I never stole, never did harm whatever but only existed quietly! Get out, leave me be!

Then came the light — a beam of blinding light falling upon my unveiled eye. It stares, but stare back I must not! For then surely will a most hideous fate befall me. A heightened rattle of breath comes from the door; a breath such as one cannot contain when one is aroused. Whatever gasping madness lurking beyond the light is surely licking its teeth, waiting to pounce. Not once before in my life did fear paralyse me so far beyond description — keeping me so dreadfully transfixed in a stupor where my body and mind are so mightily unaware of one another. I must scream; scream at the height of my lungs! Scream for help! Scream for God! For mercy!

The screams come not; I am choked by the barbed rope of fear. A horrible silhouette comes before me; leaping as abrupt as an excited crow taking flight from the gutter to find prey! I feel a tremendous weight strike the whole of my body. I feel — by God! — I feel the phantom nails of Death greedily gripping after my breath!

She Is

Millie Turner

When they buried me,

My mum was angry that I'd kept it in for so long,

She would ask and ask,

In hope that,

My corpse would revolt in an answer,

A reply,

But my secrets had metastisised into a malignant grip that
pulled me through ashes and into
soil,

Yet,

I was no Phoenix,

I was born from fire,

In my fierce mother's womb,

But *my* limbs didn't turn to swords when bitten like hers do,

All I caught was her iron curtain like a cold in Spring,

And she is the template I pull over every act,

The pattern my scales need when afraid,

The breath to every drowning mistake.

Inappropriate Contemplations

Hanna Zubarev

My time keeps running out. It perishes before my eyes, and wipes clean the mess it made with its crumbs and its stickiness. It betrays me, trying to convince me that there is enough, that the sandbox is full and contained with no cracks for the opportunity of escape. I don't believe it. You are a fragile friend who wishes to get rid of me, to live on your own without the unnecessary stress I implement upon you. Your mechanisms are far too complicated to understand how blinks transform into decades, how fast you run. I continue to fall short, with every effort to negotiate a settlement for stability. My dear friend laughs in my naive face and only runs faster. I have found there is no negotiating with you. No means for containment. No accessibility to flow with your current, be it far from human grip. I cannot understand this feeling I have, why I feel so close to death. This catatonic sensation which cripples my wellbeing and screams at me in the middle of the night to stop wasting the time which limits itself so heavily. A sleepless beauty which awaits a kiss from the grim reaper, only to find disappointment in his allegiance to you. Leaving me trapped, surrounded by thick glass, standing on an island of sand as it continues to trickle onto my head, leaving less and less space for breath. Paralyzed, I find no comfort in this deep sleep, no pleasure in witnessing my very skin wrinkle and droop further towards the floor. In fact, it is horrifying. I tremble at the thought of your capabilities and the lack of mercy you show. Insensitive to any circumstance, I fear how reckless you are. You play with yarn and clip when you desire, no measurements, no calculations, no pity. These games you play, such strange games, I do not understand how fingers of silver can tremble so violently. How you can summon a black hole in a mind which has seen you for far too long. I do not understand how we forget you so often. The tick of each second is recorded, examined, and placed into a file. Each file in its own box with its own name in its own designated space in your library. I wonder how long you have witnessed each transformation, as I am convinced you existed far before our estimations. I simply cannot comprehend this illusion you cast over us all, again, I don't believe you. I don't believe you are here to remind us to stay present, or to cherish the limits of our existence, or even to give us an understanding of our place in this god awful world. I think you are a trickster, and a bloody good one for that matter. I think you have tricked us all into worshipping you day and night, hand-cuffed at the wrist, an explosive arrangement of numbers, constantly dictating our every move. We have set names for your particles, cheering with gratitude at each year you have watched us suffer with laughter. Presenting presents of materialistic value for losing yet another grasp of your intangible consequences. I wonder how far you stretch and if you will ever face breakage. I wonder if you are a puppeteer or a puppet, I wonder who is pulling the deviant strings, is it you? I haven't figured out if I am angry with you or my own unsuccessful endeavors, or are you the reason for their failure, or am I just finding excuses to settle the lack of contentment within me, or am I being foolish for even assuming there is a correlation, but there must be. There must be. I tell myself, correlation does not imply causation. But then how do I justify this guilt of emptiness, this lack of? How do I settle my spastic nerves from erupting and involuntarily awakening a pyroclastic flow which coats my physical self and molds me into a rigid nobody with a hollow interior? What shall I do to preserve this very moment without permanently solidifying its existence and inadvertently confining myself to only its surroundings without reach of every other movement, without flexible potential, and hold sight solely of what's in front of me? Why does the hippocampus choose one over the other? Why do some memories merely pass by and others dreadfully haunt my waking life? The riddles you dispense, if I shall call them that, are melting every ounce of patience inside me. My dear friend, please let go of your grip from my lungs. Though your clench has allowed me to be in full awareness of each breath, and for this I am grateful, sometimes I long to forget, if only for a short time, that I am temporary, that this all will soon be a dusty file on the highest degree of your catalogue. Perhaps this request is beyond your control, as it is me who accepted your psychotic handshake to begin with, and it is me who allowed my organs to be raped by your illusions, but years have passed and I am no better off. This misunderstanding of you, of which I cannot elaborately articulate entirely in my liking, has prevented me from a comfort I've seen in others. Though sometimes I do doubt the totality of these inappropriate contemplations, as often I witness myself flying above the horizon, observing the very nature of human despair, and in the blissful breeze that cuts through my body and awakens me with a rather lonesome coldness, I understand that you are not all bad. I understand your lack of attachment is not particular, as your shoulders are bare of any guilt-full weight, and with this I cannot hold you accountable. Though still I hold a disliking towards my relationship with you, and am only filled with an acute anxiety after unintentionally obsessing over you in a single sitting. I am uncertain whether these contemplations are viewed as ludicrous, though I believe them to be not, and am highly curious how often they protrude into other's minds, as I am convinced this is an issue for humanity and not solely myself. I am aware of my maddening fixation on your mighty powers, perhaps because I wish to understand their mechanical workings, and still I have to remind myself of the lack of association between our human clocks and you. There is nothing mechanical about you, and this is the premise which leaves me hanging on such a thin string, because I simply don't even know what that means. I don't know if I agree. I understand the ouroboros nature of your existence, concluding into itself and disgustingly reappearing with no point of separation. Within this loop, we find delineations which allow us, to some degree, to understand in which rotation we now breathe in. Though my perplexed mind, filled with disturbance, rather desires to know of your mysterious venom, the consequences of your absent tail, how far your tongue can reach, what your hiss sounds like. These secrets of yours, which coat every question in the ways in which I live my life, are there only to bother and frolic the essence of my character. This is why I am uncertain of your mechanisms, because they are more intricate and tangled than what appears at face value. Your secrets are only observable with a fine microscopic lens, taking years to obtain. And here I go again, how to speak of you without the paradox of the meaning we played upon you. How do I even dare to try to explain these starving, poorly-fashioned, and rightfully irritating thoughts? Though here I am again, in the darkness of my room, thinking about you, as I always do, and having this undesirably piercing pain, in which the sole remedy for quieting my mind, is simply to sleep. Until the break of dawn I have, to rest without the excruciating pressure of convulsing from my affirmation of your presence, and still, it is never enough time.

Double-Slit Experiment

Olivia Shannon

spinning electrons

well-orchestrated
as the event of myself
reverberating

in the dark matter
the non-matter
the experience
which is not physical

black holes swinging
galaxies like halos

there is no beginning
only right now
this moment—

gravity capitulates
at event horizons

there is no beginning
observers are one
with the observed —

time turns and returns
in symmetries of silence

there is no beginning
observers are one
with the tectonic grip
of all that is —

our instruments
create their findings

Death in the Afternoon

Deirdre Maher

The day Granddad died, Aisling O'Riordan came to tea. I had never had a friend to tea in my life. Back in Canada, I had never had a friend.

On my first day at St Enda's, Aisling had marched over at break time with an extra bottle of milk and shoved it at me. 'So, Sister Emily says you're over from Canada,' she said. 'Say somethin' then.'

'Like what?'

She shrugged. 'Anythin'.'

I searched my brain for something interesting to say.

'My goldfish died. It kinda jumped outta the bowl.' I offered.

She nodded and called out to a small group of girls behind her. 'She DOES have an accent, Elaine!'

One of the girls made a face at me as Aisling took my arm and we linked up together.

'Jesus,' she said, 'They're pathetic. Did ye flush it down the toilet?' she went on. 'The goldfish, I mean. My brother Darren did that to ours, only it wasn't dead. My Mam was ragin' with him. He just wanted to see did it swim back up again.'

'Did it swim back up again' I asked.

'It bloody didn't. Poor Darren. She leathered him. Have you a brother?'

'No.' My tummy started to hurt, the way it always did when I remembered Mikey. 'No, I don't,' I said again.

It was Aisling who told me the facts of life. She heard them from her big sister Nikki. She told me one day as we were lounging on her bed in the room they shared, flicking through Nikki's *Jackie* magazines, surrounded by posters of David Cassidy and Marc Bolan.

'That's disgusting.' I said when she told me. 'My Mom and Dad would never do that.'

'I'm tellin' ye, it's true. Nikki says. But I dunno, she could be messin' with me. I mean, I can't see my Da puttin' his thing in my Ma's –'

'Stoppit!'

Aisling giggled and sat up. 'Yeah, she's probably messin' with me. She's a right pain in the arse.'

It was my turn to giggle. Nobody swore in our house.

Aisling had lots of friends and I knew I was just one of them, but more than anything I wanted to be her best friend. Before I came along, she was best friends with Elaine Sheehy. I was always having to share her with Elaine. So the day Aisling came to tea was extra special because I had her all to myself.

When we got home to my house, Mom told us to go outside to play, because Granddad was having a nap. His room was downstairs with a big window looking out over the front garden.

'Stay away from the front of the house now, and keep the noise down.'

We started to play our "Dares" game. I loved this game. There wasn't much I wouldn't do to look good in front of Aisling. She had just climbed over the back wall from our neighbours' garden, after rescuing one of their garden gnomes, when Mom came outside. I watched Aisling hide the gnome behind an overgrown shrub. I could still see the tip of its bright blue painted cap through the branches. I was so scared that Mom would notice the gnome that it was a couple of minutes before I realised she was telling Aisling to go home.

'But she hasn't had her tea yet!' I clenched my fists. I could feel my nails digging in to the palms of my hands.

'Don't use that tone with me. Granddad doesn't feel well,' she said. 'I'm afraid Aisling will have to go home. Don't start that, Cora.' she turned without another word and went back to the house.

Aisling looked at me, 'Your face has gone all red. Are ye all right?'

I could feel my cheeks burning. Breathing heavily, I nodded and slowly unclenched my fists.

'Time for a dare?' she asked. 'I dare ye climb up and spy on your Granddad!' She challenged, 'Scared of your Mam?' as I hesitated.

'No!' I lied. We crept round to the front of the house until we were standing in front of Granddad's window. The top of my head barely reached the windowsill. I tried to pull myself up, but I kept sliding down and scraped my knee in the process. It hurt like hell, but I wasn't going to let on.

Aisling gave me a considering look. 'I'll let ye off,' she said, 'I'll do it. You give me a leg up.'

I bent and clasped my fingers together. Aisling gripped the stone sill and put one foot in my waiting hands, then heaved herself up to the window. I staggered beneath her weight and felt the grittiness of the dirt from her shoe on my palms.

'Hold steady!' She shaded her eyes with her hand and peered inside. 'Your Mam's beside the bed. She's leanin' over. She's... she's... quick, help me down! She's comin'.' Her feet landed with a smack on the driveway and she steadied herself against me.

'Did she see you?' I knew Mom would murder me for this.

'No! I don't know. Listen, I'll have to go. Ye better go inside. I'll see ye tomorrow at school.'

She ran off down the drive. I didn't want to go back inside but I knew I had to. I opened the back door and tiptoed into the kitchen. Mom was sitting at the table, staring in front of her. She had her sad Mom face on. My tummy started to hurt. On the table lay the wig she wore when there were other people around. I hated to see her head like that, those big bald patches. She didn't seem to notice me at all. I tried to stay invisible, tried to slip past her to the hallway. She looked up. I held my breath. Had she seen us?

'He's dead. Your Granddad's dead.'

She said it like it was my fault. Maybe she thought it was.

'Will Daddy come home now?' I asked her.

Mom looked at me like she had never heard anything so stupid and I began to cry. She sighed. 'I have to call the doctor now. Don't start, Cora. Daddy will come for the funeral, and you'll see him then.'

Next day at school, Mom came with me into the classroom. She made me stand up beside her at the teacher's desk while she told Sister Emily about Granddad and about the funeral happening the next day. I was mortified. I could see Elaine smirking and Aisling had a funny look on her face. It was even worse when Mom left.

'Sit down, dear,' said Sister Emily, bending over me, her round face so close I could see the whiskers on her chin. 'Now class, we must all be very nice to Cora today. A very sad thing has happened. Her Granddad passed away yesterday into the arms of the Lord. Let's say a prayer now for the repose of his soul.'

I tried not to look at anyone, I was so embarrassed, but I couldn't help notice Aisling making weird faces at me and mouthing something which might have been, 'Oh! My! God! Are ye ok?'

I started to feel a little better.

At break time she and Elaine dragged me out to the yard. We stood in the shade of an apple tree.

'Sorry about yer granddad, Cora,' Aisling said. 'What happened to him?'

'I don't know,' I told her. 'I think he had a heart attack. He just was dead when Mom went in to him yesterday.'

A quick look passed between them.

'What?' I asked. 'What's wrong?'

Aisling hesitated.

'I'll ask,' said Elaine. 'So, Cora, tell us, has your Mam got the cancer?'

'What? No. What do you mean?'

'I mean that Aisling saw your Mam take her wig off yesterday,' said Elaine. 'When yez were spyin' on your Granddad and now we know he was there dyin'.'

'Shut up, Elaine,' said Aisling. 'Why didn't ye say anythin'?'she asked me, 'Aren't we friends?'

'I didn't say anything because she doesn't have cancer,' I said.

'Why has she no hair then?' asked Elaine. 'My Aunty Mary had the cancer and all her hair fell out. Is your Mam dyin'?'

'Like you'd care!' I said to her and turned to Aisling. 'It's not cancer. It just started to fall out.'

'Jesus, does that even happen? Yer hair just falls out?' Aisling tugged at her blonde ponytail.

I nodded.

'Your poor Mam. I didn't know what to think - one minute she had a full head a' hair and the next she whipped off the wig. Jesus, I nearly died with the shock. Sorry Cora, no offence. Your poor Granddad and everything. Lookit, we'll look after ye today — won't we Elaine?'

'Wha'? Yeah, 'course.' Elaine sniffed and glared at me behind Aisling's back but I didn't care. I linked arms with Aisling.

'So her hair just fell out?' she asked me as we went to collect our break time milk.

'I think it's when you get old and you don't have enough vitamins.' I was making it up now but how could I tell her the truth without telling her about Mikey? 'It's called "a low peesha" or something like that.'

'Jesus, we better drink our milk then lads,' said Aisling.

Funerals happen fast in Ireland. I don't remember too much about Granddad's funeral now. Standing in the graveyard, looking down at the shiny brown coffin at the bottom of a great hole of dirt, Daddy holding my hand too tight, Mom like a statue beside him. I knew we were all thinking about another funeral.

Back at the house, I clutched my sticky glass of coke and tried to make myself invisible. It wasn't hard. It was like the grown-ups didn't want to see me. There weren't many people there, neighbours and some old men who knew my Granddad, boring on about the old days and eating sausage rolls and curly sandwiches my Mom made. One man nodded and smiled at me. Afterwards, I asked Mom who he was.

'That's Dr Sheehy,' she said. 'Remember? He came to the house the day Granddad passed away. He's a friend of your father's. Isn't his little girl in your class?'

Daddy stayed longest. He tucked me in at bedtime and I tried hard not to cry. That always made my tummy hurt more. Afterwards, I crept to the top of the stairs and crouched to listen, hugging my knees. Looking down, I could see Daddy's bald patch was getting bigger.

'It was good of you to take care of Pops,' I heard him say to Mom.

'He took care of us in his own way, when we came back. Somebody had to.'

Now they would argue again, I thought. Instead, Daddy nodded.

'I know,' he said. 'How has she been?' By "she" I knew he meant me.

She shook her head. 'I never know what she's thinking. She seems to have made friends at school, at least.'

'That's good,' he said.

When he left, I knew it was because of me.

I fell asleep at last and dreamt about Mikey. I saw his face again, under the water as clear as the day he died. In my dream he swam to the surface but before he could reach me, I woke up. Through the darkness I could hear Mom crying and I buried myself under the blankets and put my fingers in my ears. I couldn't wait to get back to school.

When I saw Aisling in the school yard I waved and started over in her direction, but then I saw Elaine take her arm and they went into school together. Hadn't she seen me? All through first morning lessons I tried to get her attention, but she didn't look my way.

At break time I hurried over to where they stood together under the apple tree in the school yard. As I came up to them, Elaine nudged Aisling.

'Here she is with her "a low peesha". Didya ever hear the like?' Aisling was silent.

'My Mom does so have "a low peesha".'

'Well, maybe she does,' said Elaine, 'But my Da says your Ma's "destroyed with the grief" and that's why her hair fell out.'

I went cold all over. Aisling wasn't looking at me.

'I thought we were friends, Cora.' Her voice was low.

'What's wrong, Aisling? We are friends, aren't we?'

'Friends don't tell lies. Not to each other. I'm not talkin' about your mother's hair. You lied about havin' a brother. And don't tell me you don't have one, cos I know ye had a little brother and I know he died. Elaine found out from her Da and she told me. Why did ye not say?'

Elaine broke the silence. 'I know why.' Her voice was sure, steady. We both looked across at her.

'It was your fault, wasn't it?' she said. 'That's what my Da heard. I heard him tellin' my Ma. Your brother was only little and he drowned and it was your fault?'

'It's not true! It wasn't my fault!' I stammered. 'I'm sorry Aisling. I did have a brother. I'm sorry I didn't tell you before. I just couldn't. I didn't want to spoil everything.' Tears ran down my cheeks. 'You don't understand. Mikey was perfect. Not like me. Everyone loved him. I loved him too, but when Mikey was around, everything was different. I didn't mean to hurt him, I wouldn't!'

Aisling's face went white and she took a step back. I tried to explain.

'It was an accident. Thursday afternoons Mom brought us to the pool. It was just the little pool, I was just playing with him, Aisling, just messing with him.' I swallowed. 'Then he was under the water, and he didn't come up. I waited and he didn't come up, and then I screamed and screamed and they came and took his body out...'

'Stop. Stop.' said Aisling. 'It was your fault.' She was crying now too.

The bell rang and they walked away together, leaving me alone under the apple tree.

'Aisling!' I called after her. She kept walking. 'I only wanted to see did he swim back up again,' I whispered.

Four Doors

Kelly Squires

She built the four-door house to hide
For escape
But the fourth door doesn't open

She built the house from memory
of a story of a man
who turned himself to fin and scale
and was caught in his own net
In truth, she built it to escape the safety
Of a family that she never wished for

One door is fixed in space
like any door
And one door shows the place
where the house itself stands:

A plain of steam and ice and running water
The delicate point that balances
states of matter, locations
like the repelling ends of magnets
held fast, facing one another,
building an outward energy
that has never been released —

this house could be a weapon

One door can lead anywhere
It only exists when it's needed
Most and least reliable of the four,
it can come to your rescue
But it's a weakness
After all,
you don't need to know where it is
only how to call it

That door steals her sleep some nights
or stands uneasy at the back of dreams
Every time she swears she'll seal it off
but it's the only one that's served its purpose

The last door doesn't open

The house was built with a prayer
That she never dreamed
would come to anything
She shivers to think
that if it was a prayer
someone must have answered

Prequel to "The Tell-Tale Heart" by Edgar Allan Poe

Katie Swan

Carefully — the man touched the wet brush to my nose, his pale blue eye watched me with such intent — so intently — that it made the tiny box in my chest, that imitated that of a heart, grow louder. The eye brought me great discomfort, but I loved the man... So, I grew to love the eye. He stood back, his sickly eye examining me — he smiled and thrust the paintbrush into a water pot and moved me from the table top to the floor. I had never seen such glee in a man as he danced around the workshop, his bulbous cheeks red with delight. I watched him as I stood, idle, my arms pointlessly hung by my sides. The man turned back to me, 'You are complete!' he lifted me up and spun me round.

Years, since then, had passed. The man was older — much older — now, and his passion had faded. I had grown to be known as his son; a son who needed paint ever so delicately reapplied to my surface every few months to maintain likeness — but the old man hadn't held a brush in months. Although, I had held the very same paintbrush that created my features, to try and replicate the man's work but I never got it quite right — my reflection never seemed the same. I stood on the planks by the man's bed, the very same planks from whence I came, and tucked the sheets around him. The man gave little recognition to my presence, only opening his eyes and reaching out to remind me of the work to be done. His quiet voice fell on deaf ears — that eye — that cursed eye that created me with such attentiveness, it made my blood run cold, my fists held the sheets in balls. Only did my box start beating again once he reclosed his eyes.

My hatred grew for the man, but mostly for his eye — that wretched thing — I wished nothing but to have a companion, something the man had been until he abandoned me and his craft for greater things. If you had cared for somebody the way I cared for the man, you would understand that I wish not to hurt him — but the walls of this old house that I once called home had become a cage — a cage in which I could only escape if I were to follow through with one thing. My fingertips buzzed at the thought — no, no I did not want to kill the man. It was the eye — I needed to be free of the damned eye that imprisoned me. I called to him in a cordial tone, maybe today his attention would be on me once again — for I had not always hated that eye. The sound of shoes on wooden steps told me that he had heard my call, he was awake, he had passed the night once again — oh if only he never cared to wake.

Lady Lazarus in Color

Olivia Johnston

The oven kept on going. Just a pinch of a granulated family, a
dash of inner turmoil, I was always told that brilliant people
suffer. For what?

I stood in the kitchen, getting a cup of sea water. They had a
large oven, it kept on going. Going, going, going. That terrible
thing made beautiful pastries I ate daily, apple tarts and red,
red hearts just like mine. Devastating experiences make ruby
red hearts, just like the oven, that made me sick yet satisfied me
with fruity delicacies.

I wanted to make some hot chocolate for my children, they held
my hands tight as I stirred the whole milk.

The oven steamed and kept going. What was it even making
that made it smell so obscene today? I don't remember. My sea
water tasted odd as well, it was sweet and blameworthy. Who
was to blame for its sweetness? The sea water company? The
packaging? The sea? Me? Me... that sounds about right, and
the oven kept on going. Why is my red heart sweet, why is
poetry the sea water I drink and drink so poignant in sadness?
I had no chocolate that day. It was gone, so was my slipping

motivation to keep this house's walls from caving. The roof was already gone, the walls peeling like the unruly skin in between my cuticles that I ripped at. It reminded me of battles in WWII. This house was nothing steady, it was a war zone. This mind of mine was no home either, it was just splattered rubble from an air bomb.

The oven kept on going.

Of course, the oven. My only escape from what I have created. A life.

The Vine Within

Maria Omena

Tic-toc

I haven't heard from her today, weirdly enough. She was usually very talkative, but as I cleaned the room earlier today my head was silent. Or maybe the screams of the baby next door were drowning her voice. Either way, I welcomed it.

Today was pretty, I saw it from my window when I was cleaning. The lemony smell of the homemade cleaning solution — made of vinegar, lemon and water — made me feel like I was outdoors. The orange leaves on the trees and my yellow rubber gloves looked good together — like a ton sur ton composition of a Pantone palette. The colours outside reminded me of that day, but I don't like to think too much of it. She usually has a lot to say about the subject and I am enjoying the peace.

Tic-toc

Lying here, wide awake, I wonder if I closed the tap tight enough the last time or if my hyperawareness is an omen that will save me from drowning. I don't want to drown. The thought of not being able to breathe is enough to make me breathless. Is the door locked? Yes, it is. Lock, unlock twenty-eight times plus the red velvet chair barricading it on a 45° angle, according to the markings I put on the floor. That was right before I took my seven pills with exactly 250ml of orange juice. Organic. I like taking my pills. They help me relax, especially at night when my head is in overdrive, and the tics and tocs aren't enough to block my musings. The white coats said I could take no more than six each night, but I always down seven because seven is an odd number and odd numbers have a centre while even numbers don't. Plus, seven symbolises perfection, perfection means order, order means that the tics and the tocs will be in sync. I could always take five, but five is not seven.

Back on track. After my pills I put on my light blue nightgown, the one I reserved for Mondays — sprayed three times with lavender cologne, or tea, really — prepared every other day, just 20 ml, and then I walked the twenty-eight steps to my bed. Technically. The last two are more of a jump to make the count, but I don't like to think about it. Cheat.

Now here I am staring at the low ceiling made of wooden panels, examining line by line in between them for any speckle of dirt I might have missed. There are 30 in total, and it always annoyed me that the number of lines is even. The baby starts screaming bloody murder again and I sit up, annoyed. There is no way I will be able to sleep with all this noise, pills or no pills. How can something so small be so loud?

'Just make it shut up.' I hear a groan. There she was again. 'I never left.' True.

I like to fool myself sometimes, thinking she finally got tired of me. Like a cat that lost interest in his favourite toy. She was never gone for more than a few days though, she says she doesn't want me to feel lonely. I hear my bed creaking and turn around. She is there, sitting all huddled up — her sock-covered feet showing as her pyjama trousers are pulled up.

'Did you really think I would leave you?' She looks genuinely confused, with her head cocked and her chestnut brown hair covering part of her face. 'I am not one for leaving those who matter behind. That's you, Iris, that's always been you.'

'No,' I half-groan, referring both to her visit and her words.

'Uh- yes? You know what you did, and you know it better than anyone else. I have always wondered why, though?' She parts her hair in three and starts braiding it. 'You know that you don't behave right without me. It doesn't work.'

I have always wondered about this instinct, this fight or flight that was supposed to consume me in these reluctant situations — or so I've been told. It always feels like my body doesn't understand the message my cells are trying to communicate. Some say fight, some say flee, but ultimately, I just freeze. She looks at me, making her wide brown eyes so young and naïve — pleading for something. Something that I can't give. I shiver.

'I felt cold too that day,' she says as an answer to the way my body hunches on itself. 'The water was freezing. And I felt thirsty even though I had swallowed a lot of water.' She bites her lip and twists her long locks, only now realising she didn't have anything to tie it with. 'I don't understand. You could have helped me. You.' Her voice is harsh, accusing. 'Why didn't you come through?'

I open my mouth, but no sound comes out of it. 'You were supposed to watch me.' Her voice is different now, more desperate, high pitched. She blames me, I don't blame her. 'Protect me, but you left me!'

Her body is a bit paler now, one can almost see the map of her veins beneath the partially translucent skin. Her lips are dry and her eyes red. Her baggy pyjamas make her seem even smaller, more childlike.

'You killed me, Iris, and you know it.' Her voice is soft like velvet again, just like I remember.

'I didn't- I didn't know.' I hear myself say, my voice stable. We've had similar conversations to this so many times and yet, I never manage to feel prepared enough for them. 'I didn't know what would happen to you. I didn't want that to happen to you.' I've told her all of that before, when you are around someone 24/7 there are only so many topics you can come up with.

'But you did know I wasn't a good swimmer. You knew you were supposed to watch me,' she spits accusingly. 'Now you get to live the life you've always wanted. But if you think that for one second, I will let you forget what you did, if you think you deserve to live without blame, you are worse than I thought.'

'I'm sorry,' I hear a voice like mine croaking, but it feels so distant. I am caged inside my own body, and I know she is right. I don't deserve to be free.

'Your apologies won't change what happened. But know, that I will still be here watching you like you were supposed to watch me. Yet unable to do anything.' She stands now in front of me, head reaching my nose. Her brown eyes piercing my skin may be metaphorical but it damn sure hurts like needles.

'I can save you. I can save us both.' I say, turning around to try to open the window behind me. It seems to be stuck, I always forget to oil these old hinges — only remembering it late at night after my hands were washed seven more times to end the day.

'You can't. It's too late for both of us,' she says as a matter of fact, seemingly unaffected. Then she coughs, as if trying to get rid of something from her lungs. It makes a gurgled sound. I see her reflection slapping her chest to get rid of whatever it is.

Then, my attention is drawn to myself again. My hair is in a neat braid, my collarbones showing through the collar of my nightgown. But that's not what caught my attention. My face twitches, and it precedes a fracture on the glass. I still can see my upper body, in the centre. But instead of seeing my pale face, with chestnut brown hair and almond eyes staring back at me — I see two.

We were inseparable, Ivy and I, I don't remember exactly when she first arrived, but she kept me company through my early teenage years. I never had many friends, people said I was weird. But she was there for me, listening to what I had to say — sympathising, encouraging, mentoring me. I welcomed her with open arms. She was always so knowledgeable, so wise. She always knew what to do and that made me feel confident in myself, with her help I could be anything and I wanted to be more like her. Who has never wished for a life without complicated decisions?

She looked exactly like me, same chestnut brown hair, same almond eyes. Her eyes were somewhat duller than mine, though. Now I recognise they were cold, but at the time I thought they made her prettier — more mysterious. Everyone loves a bit of mystery. Ivy told me not to mention our friendship to anyone; they would never understand. She was there to guard me, like an angel — and it was not everyone that had one of those. It would be our secret, bonded in blood. As we grew older, I couldn't shake her from my shadow. I was more confident, I wanted to give life a go; but she became more intrusive. She wanted to be everywhere I went, tear apart any chance I had of actually meeting people. She was suffocating me, bit by bit. Pestering me to let her take over, because she knew what to do and "I didn't know how to live right". She was a parasite, and I was trapped.

I don't remember going to the lake that day; I just woke up to the feeling of water in my lungs and those last few moments were clear as day to me. The sky was bright blue on that autumn morning. Flocks of birds were flying, migrating south for the winter that was to come. I think they were robins, I remember hearing them sing — a beautiful soundtrack for a beautiful day — what a memorable end. I remember asking myself what the hell was I doing there. I hated water and had never been a good swimmer, for that asthma was to blame.

Still, there I was. In the middle of a lake, barely able to see the shore. The current was fast, shaking me like a ragdoll, and the water was cold. I called for help, for anyone to save me. I couldn't find my footing; I was drowning.

Ivy was there; she would save me — she said.

I came to myself months later, inside a white room. I had a problem, the white coats said, but if I took those pills and stuck to the treatment, it could be controlled, and it would keep her away. Yet, she always seemed to find out where I was. They didn't understand that from that day on, Ivy never truly let me go.

Memories of You

Jenny Donath

I hugged a tree today.
Hands gliding over bark,
broken-off edges
and indentations.
My fingers yearn
to touch your skin.

Returning home,
a sea of petals,
twilight rays absorbed
in veins of maple leaves.
I want to read your hands.

I tried satisfying my hunger
with crimson apples, purple plums,
just to trace my neck
where your lips
leave me breathless.

How do I quench this thirst?
Aroma fading once mint
meets my tongue.
How can I remember
your taste?

Hazelnuts scattered on plates,
your gaze upon me.
Burnt down firewood,
"Smoke enwrap me.
Serve me as shelter
when he doesn't."

Author Bios

Sanket Alurkar

Sanket Alurkar is studying for an MA in creative writing at Kingston University. He writes short stories about travel, comedy in everyday life and poetry on his blog Writestuff. He loves reading books by Bill Bryson, Ruskin Bond, and Ernest Hemingway. He has been inspired to make people laugh and touch the audience with storytelling!

Klara Armstrong

Klara is an MA Publishing student whose writing retains a strong mental health focus. She never leaves home without a notebook and something to read, even whilst traveling around the country (and occasionally across Europe) to watch Chelsea FC. When she's not studying, she's working on her debut poetry collection.

Morgan Bratli

Morgan Bratli is a full-blooded Norwegian, but despite his Viking roots he's not here to plunder your villages. He's here to study Creative Writing and Film Cultures. He writes gothic short stories by the lamplight, and is inspired by the novels and films consumed in his free time.

Gabriella Buckner

Gabriella Buckner writes poetry and prose that draw on and twist her own experiences growing up in California. Through her work, she seeks to reveal the traumas of everyday people and to decipher the beautiful and the profound in the perfectly ordinary.

Jamie Dawson

Hello! My name is Jamie! I've been writing for most of my life. It's always been a passion of mine. As a child, I would staple pages together to create makeshift books. I recently met Rachel Joyce, the author behind this year's KU Big Read, and we discussed our love of writing, as well as our own life experiences. When she signed my copy of Harold Fry, she wrote 'Don't stop writing!' which, as a budding author, meant a lot to me. I was published in the 2019 edition of the RiPPLE for my poem 'Boy Like Me.' I love to read, some of my favourite books are Markus Zusak's *The Book Thief* and Celia Rees's *Witch Child*. I'm in my final year of my undergrad and hope to continue with my studies to become a published author someday.

Jenny Donath

Originally from Germany, Jenny is a 22-year-old undergraduate student who moved to London to pursue her dream as a creative writing student. She quickly found her passion in writing confessional poetry, discussing love, struggles, and self-growth by using nature metaphors. She also has an interest in speech writing, addressing environmental issues and animal exploitation.

Ellen Dorrington

Ellen Dorrington is a Creative Writing and Publishing student in her third year. She's interested in writing about women and their relationships with each other. When she's not reading or writing, she can be found running or at the gym lifting not very heavy weights.

Rachel Essex

Three years ago, I read *Two-by-Two* by Nicholas Sparks. Reading about the main character building up a company from nothing inspired me to go for what I wanted. I'd been writing stories, poetry and diaries since childhood, often for comfort, but that was the moment it became my passion.

Molly Hills

Having worked in an eclectic variety of jobs, Molly, now 27, studies English Literature at Kingston. With her sharp, comedic prose, she focuses on light-hearted stories centering around natural and social observations. She currently lives at home in Springfield with her husband Homer and her children Bart, Lisa and Maggie.

Rahama Hassan

Rahama Hassan achieved a First-Class Honours in English Literature and Creative Writing in 2019, and is currently pursuing an MA in Film Studies. She writes about love, humour and finding the extraordinary in the everyday. In 2017, her short story "A Summer's Day in Winter" was published in The Unseen.

Syeda Hussain

Syeda Hussain is a published author. She wrote her debut novel *Salt and Pepper: Unearthing Taboos*, under the pen name, Maria Akhanji. She is currently doing a Master's based on the second volume in the *Salt and Pepper* trilogy, titled, *BrideMaids*. Her books explore issues of child abuse, religious, and cultural dogma, that often overshadow the Muslim Asian culture.

Olivia Johnston

Olivia Johnston was born and raised in New York. She studied abroad in the fall of 2019. Olivia drew inspiration from Sylvia Plath's writing and tragic life for this biographical writing prose. It was influenced by a writing prompt for an autobiography class she took that semester in London.

Chrissie Joslin

Chrissie Joslin is a second year Kingston University student studying for a BA in English and Creative Writing. Her focal interests lie predominantly with poetry, centering largely on the depiction of mental health and the feminine ideal within that. She also enjoys exploring rhyme within her work, questioning its place, or perhaps lack of, in modern poetry.

Imogen Loth

Imogen Loth is currently in her first year studying Drama and Creative Writing. She gains inspiration from the complexity of human beings and aims especially to highlight women and their diverse stories (fictional or not). Imogen feels passionate about helping others as well as evoking emotion through her writing and aspires to publish her work as a way of reaching more people.

Dierdre Maher

Deirdre's stories and poems sometimes find homes, sometimes not. Her writing is largely fiction, drawing on her Irish roots and taking inspiration from Beckett, Joyce, Alice Munro and Lucia Berlin. She writes to have a voice in the world and to share her experience of life, love and loss.

Zoë Marriott

An award-winning young adult novelist (*Shadows on the Moon, FrostFire, Barefoot on the Wind*) Zoë Marriott lives on the east coast in the North of England, sharing her home with a manic spaniel and far too many books. She is currently pursuing her Master's in Creative Writing at Kingston University.

Caitlin Murphy

As an English and Creative Writing student, Caitlin is particularly inspired by authors like Murakami, Vonnegut and Tartt in her prose writing. She engages mostly with the area of Magical Realism; exploring the strange and the cryptic that can be found in everyday life.

Maria Omena

Maria Omena is a Brazilian poet and writer. She published her first poem at the age of six and hasn't stopped writing since. In 2016, she decided to leave her birth country and life as she knew it to study English Literature and Creative Writing at Coventry University, which led to pursuing a Masters degree in Creative Writing and Publishing at Kingston University

Esther Reynolds

I get snippets of inspirations from everywhere; conversations, songs, dreams, signage on the street, something my husband says, poetry. My biggest influence at the moment is Danielle McLoughlin, who writes about human relationships. I like to write about strange occurrences and abstract themes, something a little out of the ordinary.

Isabella Ruffatti

I am a creative writing and journalism student from the tiny Central American country El Salvador (not in Brazil) who writes to have fun, express what I cannot say and try to make sense of what goes on around me. Writing social commentary, magical realism and scripts are my pet projects at the moment. Favourite authors: Gabriel Garcia Marquez, Isabel Allende and Agatha Christie.

Dannielle Sadiq

Dannielle Sadiq is an Afro-Caribbean British writer, based in London, United Kingdom. Dannielle enjoys writing within both fantasy and autobiography genres whilst exploring her dual heritage background. She has strong interests in how the mind works and cognitive development in relation to how trauma contributes to fantasy within storytelling.

Olivia Shannon

Olivia Shannon's creative writing has won awards from Narrative Magazine, the Nick Adams Short Story Contest, the Missouri Writers Hall of Fame, and others. She holds a BA in Creative Writing from Wisconsin's Beloit College, summa cum laude, and is currently working towards an MA in English Literature.

Kelly Squires

Kelly is an MA publishing student from Orange County, California. She often draws on mythology for inspiration. "Four Doors" was the serendipitous result of mixing Norse mythology, a layman's understanding of thermodynamics, and the strange moods brought on by writing a Master's dissertation.

Anna Svensson-Stoltz

From a young age, I have written lyrics in Swedish and had a passion for music. My passion for lyrics extended into a passion for poetry. It brought me to England three years ago and this year, I decided to study Creative Writing at Kingston for a professional writing career.

Katie Swan

Katie Swan is a first-year undergraduate studying Creative Writing and Film Cultures. She has a great love for fiction and isn't confined to any specific genre or material. Katie has always loved exploring the world of creativity — from playing piano, attending drama schools, enthusing over film, to video games.

Clara Tamez

Clara Tamez is an MFA Creative Writing student at Kingston. She attended her undergraduate in Texas where she studied English and Art History. Her creative work attempts to recognize comparisons between science fiction and reality; or what is real and what could be real if the world was just a bit different.

Millie Turner

Millie Turner is a final year Journalism with International Relations student with a passion for keeping a record. Wishing to capture the zeitgeist in writing to preserve for the future. To document what has been, and what could be. Where we have gone, and what is left to explore.

Sarah Ushurhe

Sarah Ushurhe is an artist, illustrator and writer. Her graphic novel-in-progress was shortlisted for both the Laydeez Do Comics Prize and Myriad First Graphic Novel Competition. Recently, she has been commissioned as part of the first round of BBC Arts and Arts Council England's New Creatives for her art history moving image and narrative piece, which highlights the life of Fanny Eaton, a Pre-Raphaelite Model of mixed-heritage.

Leelarai Weesakul

Though I am not a prolific writer, I have written quite a few stories, poems and lyrics over the years. I often take my inspiration both from cultural and political surroundings (especially from my home country of Thailand) as well as my own journey of self-discovery.

Rebecca White

My inspirations include Kate Bush, Anne and Emily Bronte and, let's face it Shakespeare. Experimental theatre, including anything the Jamie Lloyd Company is doing at the moment; Max Porter's *Grief Is The Thing With Feathers*; my kids and their interests; alternative music and, most of all, dancing!

Hanna Zubarev

A Belarussian-American experimental writer who enjoys exploring philosophically-based texts. Inspiration is drawn from the impacts of the outside world onto the human mind and their exquisite interaction. A creative being that dives into the writing world as it changes and investigates the human condition.

About Kingston University Press

Kingston University Press has been publishing high-quality commercial and academic titles for over ten years. Our list has always reflected the diverse nature of the student and academic bodies at the university in ways that are designed to impact on debate, to hear new voices, to generate mutual understanding and to complement the values to which the university is committed.

Increasingly the books we publish are produced by students on the MA Publishing and BA Publishing courses, often working with partner organisations to bring projects to life. While keeping true to our original mission, and maintaining our wide-ranging backlist titles, our most recent publishing focuses on bringing to the fore voices that reflect and appeal to our community at the university as well as the wider reading community of readers and writers in the UK and beyond.

@KU_press

This book was edited, designed, typeset and produced by students on the MA Publishing course at Kingston University, London.

To find out more about our hands-on, professionally focused and flexible MA and BA programmes please visit:

www.kingston.ac.uk
www.ripplesubmissions.wixsite.com
@kingstonjourno